# Scout's Oath

## A Planetary Romance By
## Henry Vogel

Rampant Loon Press
Lake Elmo, Minnesota

Published in the United States of America by Rampant Loon Press, an imprint of Rampant Loon Media LLC, P.O. Box 111, Lake Elmo, Minnesota 55042. "Rampant Loon Press" and the Rampant Loon colophon are trademarks of Rampant Loon Media LLC.

www.rampantloonmedia.com

Cover artwork: Aaron Bradford Starr
ISBN: 978-1-938834-43-1 (ebook)
ISBN: 978-1-938834-44-8 (print)

First publication: February 2015

# PART I

# SCOUT'S MERIT

# Chapter 1

Callan and I lay entwined in each other's arms. Moonlight shone through the windows, casting the room into a harsh contrast of deep shadows and silver light. My gaze was drawn, as always, to my wife's face and the soft curve of her shoulder. I felt anew the wonder that this beautiful princess had fallen in love with me—a crash-landed Terran scout with no lineage and no family within fifty light-years of her kingdom.

Her beauty so captured my attention that I did not consciously notice the murmur of conversation outside our door until it stopped. We rarely had anyone come to our rooms at this late hour. My curiosity piqued, I carefully disentangled myself from Callan, pulled on some pants, and padded to the door. More out of habit than worry, I grabbed my sword before opening the door.

The guard in the hallway turned an inquiring look my way. "Yes, my prince?"

I didn't recognize this guard, but there were quite a few new faces in the Royal Guard. Captain Hunter had to replace the brave men who gave their lives defending Callan when she had been kidnapped just a few months before.

"I thought I heard voices, Corporal...?"

"Evans, Your Highness."

"Pleased to meet you, Evans. And it's just Captain Rice or, when it's just the two of us, David," I said. "I'm the prince consort, not an actual prince."

"Yes sir." Evans said nothing about voices.

"Voices, Corporal?"

"Oh, yes sir! It was nothing. Just my superior officer checking in on me." Evans flashed a smile, his eyes not meeting mine. It was obvious he didn't want to talk about it any further. Perhaps he'd gotten a bit of a dressing down.

"Very well, Evans. As you were."

Evans released the breath I hadn't realized he'd been holding. "Sorry to have disturbed you, sir."

After locking the door, I stared at it for a few seconds. I couldn't put my finger on it, but something didn't feel right.

"Are you going to stare at that door all night, prince consort," Callan said, "or come back to bed and consort with the princess?"

"The things I do to insure the royal succession..." I heaved a theatrical sigh.

"Mordan appreciates your unstinting dedication to duty."

"Only Mordan?" I asked, slipping into Callan's arms.

Callan kissed me deeply, giving me all the answer I needed.

Distracted as I was, I wouldn't have heard the door to our balcony open if it hadn't had a squeaky hinge. But the squeak drew my attention.

Someone was sneaking into our room!

# Chapter 2

I rolled out of bed, drawing my sword from the scabbard hanging on the bed post. My arm was back, ready to swing at the small figure slipping into the room when I realized who it was.

"Milo? What do you think you're doing?"

Milo put his finger to his lips. "Shhhh! Get dressed, David. Something's not right in the palace."

Behind me, I heard Callan get out of bed. Milo's eyes went wide.

Stepping in front of Milo, I said, "Callan, you're giving Milo an eyeful."

"Pish, David. Milo lived with his sister in a single room for years. I'm sure he's seen a woman's bare backside before."

Milo leaned to his right, trying to look around me. "I have, you know."

I stepped to my left to block Milo's line of sight again. "Seeing your sister's backside is not the same as seeing my wife's backside!"

The rustle of clothing came from behind me. "I'm wearing a shift now, darling. Stop worrying about what Milo is going to see and start worrying about what he is going to say!"

I reached for my clothes, nodding at Milo to fill us in.

"Things are too quiet in the palace, even for this time of night," Milo began. "And I don't recognize any of the guards."

That got my attention. As a court page, Milo was expected to know all of the guards.

Milo continued, "When I tried to come up here to talk to you, the guards at the ground floor door to the stairs wouldn't let me pass and ordered me to go to bed. I had to scale the palace wall to a third floor window to get around them."

Certain of the answer, I asked, "Was that you talking to the guard at our door a few minutes ago?"

"Yeah. He wouldn't let me knock on the door and threatened to have me beaten if I didn't clear off. I acted all scared and pretended to go away. Then I slipped through a door, onto a balcony, and got here jumping from balcony to balcony."

"Milo!" Callan gasped. "It's a hundred-foot drop from those balconies! What if you'd missed a jump?"

Milo shrugged. "I didn't."

Our hushed conversation was interrupted by the sound of a key being inserted into the lock of our door!

# Chapter 3

Whoever was outside the door was taking it slowly, trying very hard to minimize noise. Unlike the squeaky door, I doubt I'd have heard the key if I still lay within Callan's embrace.

Safe rooms had been built adjoining each of the royal bedrooms after an unsuccessful attempt to kidnap Callan when she was four years old. The doors, designed to blend in with the walls, were quite sturdy. It would take ten to fifteen minutes for a band of determined men to break one of them down. Under normal circumstances, that was far longer than it would take the alarm to be sounded and the royal guards to arrive. From what Milo had said, I suspected the situation was far from normal. I had to assume we were on our own.

"Callan, Milo, get into the safe room!" I whispered.

Callan touched a spot on the wall and a door popped open. "What about you, David?"

"I don't think we can count on the palace guards arriving any time soon," I replied. "I've got to stay out here and drive the attackers off."

"I can help!" Daggers appeared in Milo's hands. He looked like such an innocent kid it was hard to remember he'd grown up on the streets.

"No, Milo," I said. "If something happens to me, I need you to keep Callan safe."

The boy stood a bit straighter. "You can count on me!"

"I know I can. Now get into the safe room, both of you!"

For once, Callan didn't argue. The safe room door clicked shut just before the lock in the hallway door clicked open.

I took three quick steps and pressed against the wall next to the hinges of the hall door. In the moonlight, I watched the door knob slowly turn and then the door inch open. I expected light to shine through the widening crack but none did. Whoever it was obviously

6

hoped to slip into the room unnoticed and catch Callan and me unawares.

Five sword-wielding shapes glided silently in through the door, fanning out at the foot of the bed. One of the men carried a tightly shuttered lantern. It looked like they hoped to blind us by opening the lantern just as they made their move. Their plan probably would have worked, too, if it hadn't been for Milo. I no longer begrudged the boy his look at Callan's bare backside!

One of the men held up his hand, fingers splayed. He tucked in his thumb, then his little finger. It was a countdown to insure all five acted at once and with absolute surprise.

My lips curled up in a smile. Time to crash their surprise party!

*Boost!*

On the count of two, I stepped forward, grabbed the assassin with the lantern and threw him into the leader. The two men went down in a heap. The lantern rolled free, a small puddle of flaming oil pooling on the floor. I spun to my left and kicked one of the other assassins under the chin with all of my Boosted strength. His head snapped back with an audible crack. Neck broken, the assassin fell twitching to the floor.

I had hoped my sudden attack would scare off the others. It didn't. The two assassins still standing moved toward me with skill and deliberation. Backing toward the safe room door, I readied my sword and waited for their attack.

As the assassins attacked, it was obvious they had worked and trained together. They pressed their attack with a level of coordination I'd never faced in my short time on this planet. From the first cross of our swords, I was on the defensive. I was so busy parrying their attacks I was unable to mount any attacks of my own. Behind them, the leader and the lantern bearer were rising to their feet. I was hard pressed fighting two on one, I'd have no chance at all fighting four on one!

Gambling that I had learned the rhythm of the two assassins facing me, I went on the offensive. I parried an attack from the assassin on the left then lunged at the assassin on the right. My unexpected and reckless attack slipped past his guard. The point of my sword pierced his eye and drove into his brain. The assassin reeled back, screaming. The other assassin kept his attention fully on me and I just managed to jump back ahead of his next attack. Before I could take advantage of the one on one situation, the other two assassins joined him.

The three men fought with the same attention and coordination I'd been facing from two men. I was sorely pressed keeping these three assassins at bay. My sword flashed and I danced back and forth just ahead of their blades. I found no openings for attack and knew I'd never get away with the surprise attack I'd used seconds before.

The leader sized up the situation and grinned. "Just be patient, lads. He can't keep this up for more than a few minutes. He'll tire and then we'll have him!"

# Chapter 4

The leader of the assassins was right. I might hold these men off for several minutes, but one of them would get past my guard or I'd eventually suffer Boost Burnout. My only hope was to take as many of them with me as possible. I prepared to attack, planning to ignore defense entirely and concentrate on killing these three men. I fully expected to die from the wounds they would inflict.

Then I heard the door open behind me.

"Callan!" I said. "That door is going to be your only protection in a minute or two! Shut and bar it!"

"Don't be daft, darling," Callan said, her voice rock steady. "And could you stand in one place for a second or two?"

I had no idea what she had in mind, but the eyes of the assassin leader had gone wide as Callan spoke. I did as she requested.

I heard a sharp snap over my shoulder and a crossbow bolt buried itself between the eyes of the assassin leader! The confident grins vanished from the faces of the remaining assassins.

"Don't let those two escape," Callan said. "This crossbow is devilishly hard to wind!"

"Try this, Your Highness," Milo said.

"Oh, well done, Milo!" Callan said.

I heard the crossbow hit the floor then Callan said, "Darling, duck!"

I dropped to one knee. The assassins looked perplexed. Then the Onesie whined and the assassin who had pretended to be a guard flew back against our bed. The gun had punched a fist-sized hole through his chest.

I'd hoped the remaining assassin would run, giving me a chance to capture and question him. I had no such luck. The sudden reversal of fortune unnerved him. He panicked and attacked wildly. Unable to disarm him, I ran the man through.

I dropped Boost then swept Callan and Milo into a fierce hug. "I'd have died if it weren't for the two of you!"

"I picked the Onesie out of your pocket when you stood in place so Callan could shoot the crossbow," Milo said. "I hope you don't mind."

"You did fine," I said, tousling his hair.

"Winding the crossbow took so long!" Callan said, her calm beginning to unravel now that the fight was over. "I was afraid I wouldn't be—"

I interrupted her with a kiss, "That was quick thinking, dear! I didn't even know there were weapons in the safe room."

The assassin I'd run through groaned. He wasn't dead!

Dropping next to him, I caught his head in my hands. "Who hired you? Were you trying to kill us or capture us?"

"W-water..."

Milo ran to our bedside table and grabbed the water pitcher kept there. I poured a trickle of water into the man's mouth.

"T-thanks." He licked his lips. "K-kill you. Capture princess. Already have parents."

Callan gasped at that. Her parents had been out of the country on a diplomatic mission. They were expected back tomorrow afternoon.

"Who hired you?" I asked again.

The man shook his head, refusing to answer. He'd just given up what he had to see the anguish on our faces.

"We don't need him to tell us anything else, David." She looked into the eyes of the dying man. "It can only be Ardhan Windslow. This kidnapping attempt is just like the one he planned sixteen years ago. Tell me I'm wrong, assassin!"

I glanced from the assassin to Callan. The rising emotions of a moment ago were gone. Her face was hard and her eyes were as cold as the depths of space. Under her glare, the assassin nodded.

Without another word, Callan stood. "Milo, find Martin and bring him up here. Tell no one else what has happened."

Milo nodded and dashed out the door.

"You're not going to summon the guards?" I asked.

10

"No," she said, striding to her wardrobe. "My parents lives may depend on secrecy. Having a couple of dead assassins found in our room will help, too!"

# Chapter 5

"I'm sure you've come up with a great plan," I said, "but could you explain it to me?"

Behind me, the dying assassin convulsed, gurgled, and breathed his last.

"Windslow hired these men to kidnap me," Callan replied, "so I'm going to let him think his men got me. We leave a couple of bodies in the room—testament to your abilities—then we slip out of the palace without letting anyone else know we're leaving. The logical assumption will be that we've been kidnapped. We'll have a day or two before Windslow figures out what really happened. We've got to use that time to find my parents."

"Won't that leave the country in chaos?"

"That's why our first stop is going to be my uncle's fief. I'll send him back here to take the throne until we get my parents back. It's a long shot but Windslow hasn't had a lot of time to plan or prepare for this. If we put our minds to it, I think we can figure out where he's holding them."

"What's Martin's part in all of this?" I asked.

"The same as it was when the trogs took the city of Faroon," Callan responded. "I need a fleet for the search and involving the navy would tip our hand to Windslow. Besides, I'll need to be directly involved if this plan is going to work, and the navy would insist on keeping me out of harm's way."

"I want to keep you out of harm's way, too!"

"I know, David. But I won't have to argue with you like I would the admiralty." She tilted her head and batted her eyelashes.

I sighed. "Which bodies do you want to leave in our room?"

Callan and I spent the next several minutes setting the scene in our room.

"My but you two have been busy!" Martin said as he and Milo slipped into the room. Martin winked. "And you've killed five assassins, too!"

Callan didn't even crack a smile. "I need you to gather a fleet for me again, Martin."

"Um, correct me if I'm wrong, but aren't we in the palace? Don't you have a whole navy at your command?"

"Did Milo fill you in on the situation?" Callan asked. At Martin's nod, she continued, "What do you think will happen if I go to the Royal Navy with this?"

Martin grimaced, "Hours wasted while the naval brass debate and dither and make plans. You'd be placed under heavy guard and end up trying to command a search of the north country from the palace."

"Right. Windslow would see the navy coming from miles away. He'd cut his losses, kill my parents, and disappear." Callan's voice flattened. "I won't let either one of those things happen!"

"If you want it kept quiet, I'll need hard currency to hire the ships. Money buys silence—credit, not so much." Martin glanced around the room. "Have you got much money in here?"

"I don't have any money," Callan replied. "That's what the exchequer is for."

"I'll have to remember to get an exchequer of my own when this is all over." Martin smiled without humor. "But that's going to make it a lot tougher to hire ships quietly."

I shook my head. "No it won't."

"Care to enlighten a poor Scout Second Class, Rice?" Martin growled.

"It should be obvious to a former raider like you." I turned to Milo. "Are you interested in robbing the Mordanian treasury, kid?"

# Chapter 6

Milo's eyes went wide, a grin split his face, and his head began nodding so fast I was afraid it might come loose!

"David, that's brilliant!" Callan beamed at me.

"Yeah, brilliant," Martin groused, "until Milo gets caught breaking into the treasury. He's a talented pickpocket, David, but you're asking him to break into one of the most secure rooms in the country!"

"He won't need to break in, Martin." Callan sat at her desk and began writing. "This note will get him inside."

Martin read the note over Callan's shoulder. "I've seen your tiara, Callan. It's a lovely antique but it doesn't have enough gems to cover the ships we'll need."

"The tiara is just Milo's excuse to get into the treasury." Callan folded the note and sealed it with her signet ring. "Once he's inside, Milo gets to prove to us just how good a thief he is! There are plenty of jewels to choose from, Milo. We'll have to trust your professional judgement."

Milo took the note from Callan. "Are there cut gems in the treasury?"

Martin clapped Milo on the shoulder. "Smart thinking, lad." Seeing our confusion, he said to Callan and me, "Jewels are distinctive, which makes them harder to sell and worth less money. Gems are easier to carry, easier to sell, easier all around."

Callan nodded her understanding. "I always wondered why the spymaster kept all those loose gems down there. How much will we need to hire the ships?"

"Err on the side of excess, Milo," Martin advised. "A big fistful would be perfect."

"Speak to Nist and Tristan before you rob my treasury," Callan said to him. "If he can, I'd like Nist to fly the *Pauline* to my balcony in two hours. I don't want to risk anyone catching sight of us as we leave the palace. I want Tristan along in case my parents need medical attention after we rescue them."

Milo nodded and slipped out the door.

Martin moved to follow him. "I'd best get started hiring ships. I'll come back on the *Pauline* to pick up the gems."

The waiting chafed on both of us. We ended up staring at a two hundred year-old framed map of Mordan hanging on the wall of our room, trying to remember where modern cities stood and guess where to concentrate the search. It was almost a relief when someone knocked on our door.

Almost.

Motioning Callan out of sight, I drew my sword and opened the door a few inches. Outside stood Captain Hunter, the man in charge of the royal guard. One of his big hands gripped Milo by the neck.

"Captain Rice," Hunter said, "I must speak with Her Highness. I'm afraid I've caught a thief!"

# Chapter 7

"You may leave the boy with me, Captain Hunter," I said. "I'll see that he's suitably punished. What was he stealing?"

"Gemstones." Hunter craned his neck, trying to see past me into the room. "Where is Her Highness?"

"Indisposed. We were sleeping when you knocked."

"You sleep with lanterns lit? And where is your guard?" Suspicion clouded Hunter's face. "I must insist upon seeing Her Highness. Now."

"You'd best let him in, David," Callan said, stepping next to me. "But before you enter, Captain, I must request and require that you remain quiet and do nothing until I have a chance to explain what you will see."

Hunter's eyes widened, but he never hesitated. "I accept and accede, Your Highness!"

I swung the door open and Captain Hunter stepped into our room. If his eyes had widened before, they fairly bulged out at the sight of the blood and the bodies.

"I must alert the guard!" Hunter exclaimed. "I must—"

"Do nothing until you hear my explanation—as you swore just seconds ago!" Callan's voice was a whip crack.

Hunter straightened to attention, "My apologies, Your Highness! It's just..." He waved his hand around the room.

"I understand your reaction, Captain, but I cannot allow you to follow your first impulse," Callan said. "My parents' lives may depend upon you doing the exact opposite."

It took but a moment for Callan to bring the captain up to speed.

"My apologies for suspecting you, Captain Rice," Hunter said.

"Never apologize for making Callan's safety your priority," I replied.

16

Hunter nodded once. "But I am not sure about this plan, Your Highness. It seems very risky."

"That's because it *is* very risky, Captain," Callan said. "But I believe it's the best chance we have to save my parents!"

"And what does your husband think of your involvement?" Hunter asked.

"My husband hopes to convince me to stay at my uncle's fief," Callan replied.

I hadn't said any such thing, but Callan's assumption was correct.

"Am I going to succeed?" I asked.

"It's doubtful."

"You know I'll have to try anyway."

"Yes, darling. I'd be hurt if you didn't."

"Best of luck with that, Captain Rice," Hunter interjected. "But, Your Highness, you indicated I had a part to play in this plot of yours. What did you have in mind?"

"I'd like you to be the one to raise the alarm, Captain Hunter," Callan replied. "Having the captain of the Royal Guard discover my supposed kidnapping will add just the right touch of veracity to our deception. Though you must wait until we're long gone from the palace before doing so."

"If you think that's best, Highness, I shall do just that."

"Thank you, Captain," Callan said. "Return to your normal duties. Give us two and a half hours, then come 'discover' our disappearance."

Captain Hunter saluted, started for the door, then paused. Fishing a small bag from his pocket, he handed it to Callan. "I suppose you'll be needing these gems the lad was...I suppose *stealing* isn't the right word here."

After Hunter was gone, I looked at Milo. "What happened? How did Hunter catch you?"

"It wasn't easy." Milo pulled a second small bag from his pocket. "I had to be really blatant before he finally realized what I was doing!"

"Wait, you got caught on purpose?" I asked. "Why?"

"Because we needed Captain Hunter to do exactly what Callan told him to do," Milo replied. "Like Callan said, it'll be more believable—especially to Windslow and his goons."

"Why didn't you mention that earlier? I could have added it to my note," Callan said.

"I didn't think about it until I was in the treasury. Captain Hunter is too duty-minded to leave his post at my request—even in your name, Callan—and I couldn't just explain the situation to Captain Hunter because he'd have raised the alarm."

"So you gave him a reason to come up here," Callan said. "Very clever, Milo!"

Milo was still basking in Callan's praise when the *Pauline* drifted up to our balcony. Martin and I loaded three of the assassins' bodies onto the airship—we planned to dump them overboard once we were well away from the city—and we boarded the little airship.

Callan looked at each of us. "Let's go find my parents!"

# Chapter 8

Two hours had passed since our rendezvous with Martin Bane's mercenary fleet. Martin, Callan, and I had devised search patterns for each of the airships involved in our hunt for Callan's parents. Each airship's captain had been paid in advance for his assistance in the search.

"I have to wait here for one more ship," Martin said as the airships left to begin the search. "It'll be here soon, but there's no reason you two should stay."

"Good," Callan said. "I need to warn my uncle about Windslow and send him back to the palace. After that we'll join in the search."

Callan's uncle, Lord Garrett, was the kingdom's designated regent should anything happen to Their Majesties before Callan's twenty-first birthday. He'd been spending more and more time in his fief as Callan's birthday drew closer. But that was before Their Majesties were taken by Windslow.

"Once Uncle Garrett is on his way to the palace to establish his regency, I'll be able to concentrate fully on my parents," Callan added.

"Did you check with your usual information sources before we left?" I asked Martin.

"Yes, David," Martin said. "I've done this before—former raider, remember? No one had heard anything about Windslow."

"What about news out of Tarteg?" I asked. "Is Raoul's mother getting back into the family business, maybe?"

"No. It's been over a month since anyone heard anything from either of them. The last news had Raoul living and traveling among the city states to the south. His mother is living quietly in a convent."

We settled a few more details, boarded the *Pauline*—fast becoming known as the princess's unofficial airship—and set course for Pingor, home to Lord Garrett. Four hours later, the dim lights of

Pingor came into view. Callan answered the challenge from the airship on patrol and we were escorted directly to Garrett's palace.

As we landed, Garrett's wife, a pale and delicate-looking woman, hurried from the palace and wrapped Callan in a hug.

"Callie, what are you doing here?" she said.

"Aunt Michelle," Callan said, "my parents have been kidnapped!"

Michelle grew even more pale, "Kidnapped?"

"Where is Uncle Garrett?" Callan asked. "I must speak with him immediately."

"You can't," Michelle said. "Garrett is being held hostage in the mine!"

# Chapter 9

Callan pulled Michelle back into a hug. "What are you doing to get Uncle Garrett back?"

"Whatever Garrett's advisors suggest, which seems to be little more than waiting and hoping." Michelle shook her head. "I wish Rob were here. He'd know what to do!"

Callan's face clouded for a moment as the pain of Rob's loss returned in full force.

"Oh, Callie, I'm so sorry! That was thoughtless of me." She took Callan by the hand and drew her toward the palace. "Come inside and tell me what's going on."

Callan told the tale in a cheery sitting room. Michelle's eyes flashed when she heard of the attempt to kidnap Callan and slay me.

"I hoped to send Garrett to Morda to establish a regency while I led the search for my parents," Callan concluded.

"If Windslow has your parents and tried to kidnap you, he's probably behind Garrett's capture as well," Michelle said.

"The timing is too convenient for it to be anything else," Callan said.

A young girl's voice came from behind a tapestry, "See? I told you Callie would bring David to rescue Daddy!"

"Ann, come out here this minute!" Michelle said. "Ellen and Brolan, that goes for the both of you, too!"

Three children came out. Ann, who was four, carried a teddy bear under one arm, wore a big smile and ran to Callan. Ellen, eight, looked as if she wanted to do the same thing but was trying to act grownup. Brolan, all of eleven, was somber, as if he was trying on the mantle of man of the house and found it heavier than expected.

"That's why you're here, right Callie?" Ann turned big eyes on me. "To rescue Daddy?"

"That wasn't why I came," Callan said, "but of course we're going to help now that we're here."

Taking a knee beside Callan, I said, "Lady Ann, you have my oath to do all in my power to rescue your father."

"I should be rescuing Da- Father!" Brolan's voice broke, ruining his pronouncement.

Michelle sighed. "David, could you talk some sense into my son?"

"Brolan doesn't suffer from a lack of sense, Lady Michelle, merely from a lack of experience." I turned to the boy. "A wise ruler delegates important missions to the person best suited for the task."

Brolan crossed his arms and looked me in the eye. "Then why are you and Callan trying to rescue the king and queen? Isn't the Royal Navy better prepared for that?"

"Yes, the Royal Navy is well equipped for search and rescue operations," Callan responded. "But there's more to consider than airships and men."

Brolan didn't back down. "Like what?"

"Brolan, how dare you take that tone of voice with Callan!" Michelle scolded.

"He's right to question me, Aunt Michelle," Callan said. "All right, Brolan, what would the Royal Navy do if I had gone to them?"

Brolan looked thoughtful for a moment. "They'd have gathered airships and made plans for the search. They'd have sent a squadron here to check on us. And they'd have put you under heavy guard."

"Very good," Callan agreed. "And what would Windslow have done when he heard about that?"

Brolan's eyes went wide. "Oh."

The two girls looked confused but Callan and Michelle gave the boy an approving nod.

"Now that we've settled that," Callan said, squeezing my hand, "promise me you'll be careful, David!"

"Careful? Doing what?" Michelle asked.

"Careful in the mine," I said. "Time is a luxury we don't have right now, so I'm going down to fetch Lord Garrett!"

# Chapter 10

Michelle gaped at me, "Don't be foolish, David! There are ten men holding Garrett. Callie, talk some sense into your husband!"

"A few minutes ago, you wished Rob were here to offer advice. What would your response have been if Rob had said that?" Callan asked.

"I'd have asked what he needed," Michelle sighed. She turned an inquiring gaze on me. "So, what do you need, David?"

"To start with, I'll need maps of the mine and an explanation of how Lord Garrett was captured," I said.

Michelle sent for maps, then gave the explanation.

"The day before yesterday, a group of former military engineers arrived in an airship and requested an audience with Garrett. They said they'd come to demonstrate a new steam drill. Callie, you know how your uncle is when he has a new mining toy to play with!"

Callan nodded and rolled her eyes.

Michelle flashed a smile which never reached her eyes. "Of course, he insisted on seeing the drill in action as soon as possible. The engineers told Garrett they were sorry, but they had to wait for their mechanic to join them because they didn't know enough about assembling steam engines. They gave some story about the mechanic having to pick up some tools in another city, insisting the mechanic should catch up with them in three or four days.

"A new drill and a steam engine to assemble? It was like dangling raw meat before a starving dog! 'I know all about steam engines!' Garrett assured them. 'I can assemble it for you.' Whoever planned this was very clever. It took fifteen minutes before they agreed to let Garrett handle the assembly.

"Garrett worked all night putting that infernal engine together. When it was finally ready, the engineers asked everyone to leave the mine. It was all for safety, they said. They'd do a test run and then call everyone back to view the results. Garrett ordered the mine cleared but insisted on staying down there himself, just in case they had trouble with the steam engine. Once Garrett's guards were clear, they took Garrett hostage. They claim to have an armed man with Garrett at all times. If we storm the mine or try to sneak in, they swear they'll know and will kill Garrett."

"How do they communicate with you?" I asked.

"The mine has speaking tubes, just like you'd find in a large airship," Michelle answered. Tears began sliding down Michelle's cheeks. "Installing them was Garrett's idea."

Callan moved next to Michelle and put an arm around her. "We're going to get him back, Michelle."

Michelle sniffed, smiling bravely. "You know that's the first time you've addressed me without 'aunt' in front of my name?"

"You'll always be Aunt Michelle to me," Callan said, "even if I just call you Michelle."

"And you'll always be the little flower girl from my wedding, Callie, even if you aren't a little girl any more."

I waited a moment while Callan and Michelle hugged. When they pulled apart, I asked, "Have they made any demands?"

Michelle snorted. "Oh, yes. They want royal pardons and more money than our fief has."

I mulled over that for a moment. "Agree to the demands."

"We can't do that, David! They'll kill Garrett when we can't deliver!" Michelle protested.

"I don't think so," I said. "If I'm right, they'll change their demands."

Michelle looked thoughtful. "I don't follow that. Please explain."

"All of their demands are nothing more than delaying tactics designed to keep you off balance and thinking about anything except rescuing Garrett," I said. "These men don't care about the ransom. They're waiting for a signal of some kind. When they get it, they'll just leave. I'd guess they're even using the steam drill to dig their own escape tunnel."

"In that case, can't we just wait for them to leave?" Michelle asked.

"For one thing, we really need Garrett to assume the regency while we search for Callan's parents," I said.

"What's the second thing?" Michelle asked.

I met Michelle's gaze. "When they don't need Garrett any more, they'll probably kill him!"

# Chapter 11

Lady Michelle was digesting what I'd said when a map of the mine was brought to me. I began studying the map, looking for something the kidnappers hadn't thought about. An hour later, I found what I was looking for.

"Lady Michelle, do you know if there are any retired miners among the staff?" I asked.

Michelle relayed the question to her majordomo. Ten minutes later, the husband of the head cook was ushered in. At my prompting, he introduced himself as Jim.

"Jim, do you know anything about the silver mine just north of the city?"

"Where them men is holdin' Lord Garrett?" he asked. "Yeah, I worked it some. Worked the copper mine t'other side o' the mountain more."

"That's what I was hoping to hear," I said. I pointed at the map. "This copper mine shaft looks like it gets very close to the silver mine—close enough for me to break through the wall. The thing is, I don't know anything about mining. Without a good guide, I'll probably just get lost."

"Copper mine's been shut up fer nigh on twenty years. Timber's prob'ly rotted out in places," Jim said. "Be dangerous."

"If I don't do something, Lord Garrett will probably die."

"Then I's yer man," Jim said. "What kinda supplies you got?"

"You tell me what you think we'll need and I'll make sure we've got it."

Jim rattled off an impressive list of items. Half an hour later, with the requested supplies loaded on the *Pauline*, Nist flew us to the entrance to the copper mine.

Swinging a heavy pack onto my back, I said, "Nist, I'll send Jim back once he shows me the shaft I'm looking for. Wait here for him, then the two of you head back to Garrett's palace."

"What about you?" Nist asked.

"I'm planning on coming out through the main entrance to the silver mine," I said as Jim and I set off for the boarded-up entrance to the old mine.

Prying the boards from the entrance proved easy—several were rotten, as Jim had predicted—then we headed in. Every inch of that mine was familiar to Jim until we came to the sinkhole blocking our path.

"Sorry, son, ain't no other tunnel goes where you wanna git." He turned toward me. "Boy, what you think yer doin'?"

I dropped the last of my gear to the ground and tied a rope around my waist. "I'm going to jump across."

"You crazy, boy? Tha's gotta be thirty foot!"

"Just find a place to tie this end of the rope, in case I don't make it" I said.

Once Jim had tied off the rope, I grabbed a pick and stepped back. *Boost*! I charged toward the sink hole and leaped out over the impenetrable darkness of the sinkhole!

# Chapter 12

My foot slipped on some loose stones as I jumped. It wasn't much of a slip, but it was enough. I knew immediately I wasn't going to make it to the far lip of the sinkhole. Worse, if the bottom of the sinkhole was closer than my rope was long, I was in for a world of hurt! Halfway across, I realized I was going to make it to the other side of the sinkhole, just not to the lip.

Maintaining Boost, I pulled my pick arm back and then drove the pick into the wall of the sinkhole. I crashed into the wall and put all my weight on the pick. It held, but I didn't want to put too much trust into such a blind swing and began looking for handholds.

"Yee ha!" Jim called. "You got guts, son. Scramble on up and tie off the rope fer me."

Yeah, that was easy for Jim to say, but I found I could dig out hand and foot holds without too much effort. Feeling more secure, I dropped Boost and climbed the wall. A few minutes later, I tied off the rope, Jim pulled himself across the sinkhole, and on we went.

Jim got talkative after my jump, filling our walk with tales of the mines and the miners. The man knew a story for every foot of that mine. A lot of them were funny and a few were tragic. It filled the time until, at last, Jim pointed to a tunnel.

"This 'un here's the one you want."

"Thanks," I said. "You head on back to the airship, now."

"Nah, I gotta see how yer gettin' through t'other mine. 'Sides, I knows where you oughta make yer hole."

I wasn't about to turn down expert advice. "Lead on, Jim!"

Ten minutes later, Jim and I used our picks to dig out a two foot deep hole in the tunnel wall. Then I pulled out the Onesie. Jim watched, curious, as I broke down the gun and set the power supply to overload. Believe it or not, the power supply overload is a design feature. Sometimes a Scout just needs to blow something up, even if it turns the Onesie into a high tech decoration. The whine of the overload was building as I placed it in the hole and scooped dirt in behind it. Grabbing Jim by the arm, I ran back up the tunnel.

A couple of minutes later, the power supply blew. Impatiently, I waited for the dust to settle. Had we blown a back door into the silver mine?

# Chapter 13

Through the settling dust, I saw the hole we'd dug was almost man-height and, when I brought a lantern to it, was relieved to see it opened into the silver mine.

"I couldn't have done this without you, Jim! But now it's time for you to go back to the airship and head home," I said. "Tell Lady Michelle to wait for me to call on the speaking tubes."

"You sure you don't need no help, son?" Jim asked. "They's got ten men."

"I've faced worse than that before, Jim, and I'm still breathing. I appreciate the offer but it's best if I go on alone from here."

"If'n you say so. But you be careful, son." Jim winked, "I 'spect that purty princess be right riled up if'n you gets hurt."

"Trust me, *not* riling my wife is always one of my top priorities!" I said.

"Them's words ta live by, lad!" Jim gave me a thumbs up and started back to Nist and the *Pauline*. I strode through the new connecting tunnel and into the silver mine.

The first thing I did was shutter my lantern until it gave off the narrowest beam of light possible. Once my eyes adjusted to the near-total darkness, I started toward the main tunnel. And almost immediately tripped over a rock. I just managed to catch myself with my free hand before the lantern could be smashed on the rocks. After that, I reigned in my desire for haste and opened the lantern's shutter a bit more. Better to go slowly with a little more light than to break the lantern and be forced to crawl with no light.

I probed the darkness ahead with my ears, hearing being the most useful sense available to me. After fifteen minutes of hearing the periodic drip of water and scuff of my boot on rock, I heard the steam drill. Five minutes later, I reached what my mental map told me should be the main tunnel. The engine sounds came from the right, farther into the mine, but the speaking tubes were to the left, closer to the surface. Where would they be more likely to be holding Garrett? I decided they'd want communication most and turned left.

Another ten minutes of careful walking and listening—the last two minutes with the lantern completely shuttered—and I was looking into the kidnappers' camp. I only saw seven of the ten men Michelle had said were down here. I assumed the other three were tending the steam drill. Garrett was tied to an iron ring driven into the left wall. As I'd hoped, he was on the end of the camp farthest from the mine entrance—the same end I was on. If luck was with me, I thought I could free him before the fighting began.

Luck was most definitely not with me. My recently sharpened hearing picked up the sound of two voices drifting up from behind me. I'd reached the kidnappers' camp just before shift change on the drill!

# Chapter 14

If I charged into the camp, I'd be silhouetted against the camp light and easily visible to the men behind me in the tunnel. It would only take one shout to alert their comrades and put Garrett's life in peril. Instead of acting rashly and charging, I rolled to the left side of the tunnel, where Garrett was bound, rose into a crouch, and slipped along the tunnel wall.

The camp's sentry faced away from me, toward the surface entrance where Garrett's men at arms were just waiting for the order to charge into the mine. The rest of men sat talking, paying no attention to anything around them. I decided to try to let Garrett know what was about to happen.

"Garrett, it's David. Rescue time is at hand," I hissed. Garrett's face sharpened into concentration. "Pull the rope taut, it'll be easier to cut. I don't have a spare sword, so run for the surface once you're free. I'll be right behind you. Do *not* wait for me."

Garrett gave a bare nod and stretched as if trying to loosen stiff joints. The rope pulled taught. I moved to within five feet of Garrett and quietly drew my sword.

*Boost!*

Jumping up, I sawed on the thick rope binding Garrett to the iron ring. The rope parted, but not before a shout rose from down tunnel. Two of the men in the camp reacted quickly, drawing swords and charging toward Garrett and me.

"Get going, Garrett," I shouted and I ran to meet the two who had reacted so quickly. They hadn't expected me to come to them so I was able to roll under their hurried swings. I slashed at the man on my right as I came out of the roll, cutting a leg out from under him. Whipping my sword around to the other man, I thrust the point into his throat. Blood fountained as I ripped my blade away. The man's hands flew to his throat and his eyes widened in horror. Gurgling, he fell away from me.

The swift brutality of my attack gave the five men within the camp reason to pause. Then we all heard the sound of running feet coming from the direction of the steam engine. Emboldened by the thought of reinforcements, the men advanced.

Charging had taken the first two men by surprise, so I figured it wouldn't hurt to try again. I ran toward the closest three men, calling, "Surrender or die!"

No one surrendered. Instead, the three men spread out, their swords held ready. From the corner of my eye, I saw a fourth man angling to get behind me. I had charged at the man in the middle, but it was time to throw off their maneuvering. I planted my right foot and dove to the left. All three men froze at my unexpected change of direction. I took advantage of their confusion and swung my sword at the man standing before me. My sword bit into flesh, opening his belly from right to left. The man screamed and clutched his gut, trying to keep his organs from spilling out. Spinning around, I found the other three men backing away.

"Surrender," a voice called, "or your lord dies!"

I turned toward the sound of the voice. Garrett lay on the ground, pinned down by a foot on his back. The sentry stood over him, his sword at Garrett's neck!

# Chapter 15

I moved my sword to my left hand and held it with two fingers. Spreading my arms wide, I concentrated on looking as non-threatening as possible. I knelt down slowly and laid the sword on the ground. As I'd hoped, all eyes were on the sword. No one saw me pick up a rock with my right hand. I raised my left arm, again using it to keep the men looking the wrong way. With a sidearm delivery, I hurled the rock at the sentry! It hit him hard on the forehead. Cursing in pain, the sentry stumbled back, freeing Garrett.

I snatched my sword from the ground and was on the sentry in an instant! Knocking his sword from his hand, I placed my sword against his throat, and dropped Boost.

"All of you, stay back or I'll kill him!" I snapped. The men stopped, stunned at the sudden reversal of their fortunes. "Garret, please get going. Michelle and your children are waiting for you at the mine entrance."

Rising, Garrett asked, "What about you, David?"

"I'll be along shortly. Send some of your men at arms when you have the chance," I said. "Oh, and tell Callan I'm fine. She's probably starting to worry."

"I always thought Callan was exaggerating when she told stories of your fighting prowess. It looks as if I owe her an apology!" With that, Garrett turned and ran toward the mine entrance.

Turning back to the kidnappers, I asked, "What now, gentlemen?"

The men exchanged puzzled looks.

"I can't afford to waste any more time on you—not even the time it will take for Garrett's men at arms to arrive," I said. "Thirty minutes ago, I blasted a hole into this mine from an old, abandoned copper mine. Take it or don't. It doesn't matter to me."

"You're not going to execute us?"

"I'm tired of killing people," I said, "but I'm sure Garrett's men will be happy to oblige you. They'll be along soon."

"What about our steam drill?" one asked.

"On behalf of Lord Garrett, I thank you for donating it to his mining operation," I smiled. "Do you have any more stupid questions?"

They shook their heads.

"One more thing," I said as they started to turn away. "If any of you ever tries something like this again, I will hunt you down and kill you. No appeal. No mercy. Do we understand each other?"

They nodded, then the man who'd been on sentry duty asked, "How do we find the way into the copper mine?"

"I'm giving you a chance to get away and now you want directions?" I waved my hand down the mine shaft, "Find it yourselves."

The unwounded men ran down the tunnel, ignoring the pleas of the man with the wounded leg and the groans of the man I'd gutted.

I ignored them as well and headed after Garrett. I met his men at arms along the way and told them the kidnappers were trying to get away through the copper mine. Unlike the kidnappers, I gave the soldiers precise directions to the connecting tunnel I'd created and they set off in pursuit.

Callan threw herself into my arms and kissed me soundly when I emerged into the morning light. Her public display caused lots of murmuring and a few disapproving looks from those gathered at the entrance. I guess that kind of thing isn't considered proper for a princess, even if she is kissing her husband. I pulled Callan close, returned her kiss with equal fervor, deciding I couldn't care less what the watchers thought of that!

As we broke off, a smudge in the sky drew our attention. I realized it was Martin Bane's airship trailing smoke as it limped toward the city!

# Chapter 16

"What's a Tartegian warship doing here?" Garrett asked.

"That's not a Tartegian ship," I said. "It's the one Martin Bane acquired as part of his deal with the Tartegian admiral"

"You're sure it's Bane?" Garrett asked. When I nodded, he pointed toward three of his patrol craft moving to intercept Martin's ship. "Then we could have trouble. After the Tartegians orchestrated your kidnapping, Callan, my men have been itching for a shot at one of their ships! They don't know Bane nor will they see much beyond the Tartegian design. I'm afraid they'll attack as soon as they're within range!"

"No!" Callan cried.

"Nist!" I yelled. "Is the *Pauline* ready to fly?"

At Nist's nod, Callan sprinted toward the airship. Following her, I called over my shoulder to Garrett, "Come on!"

"I'm right behind you, David!" Garrett said.

I bounded over the airship's railing and then pulled Garrett aboard the *Pauline*, "Is there any way to signal your airships?"

"I'll try, of course, but all of their attention is going to be on their target."

Grabbing a couple of colorful flags, I handed them to Garrett. He positioned himself in the bow of the *Pauline* as the little airship rose into the air. Nist brought the engines to full power, worked the ailerons, and put the ship into a steep ascent. Over the roar of the engine, Callan filled her uncle in on the attack against us, what little we knew of her parents, and who we believed was behind everything.

His arms still waving frantically, Garrett said, "It appears you've accrued another debt of thanks that my family owes you, David."

"Uncle, David is part of your family, too. He has been for nearly a month!" Callan smiled and slipped an arm around my waist.

"Forgive me, my boy," Garrett said. "I'm still adjusting to the idea that the niece I spoiled so horribly is a married woman, now."

Callan rolled her eyes. "You and Daddy, both!"

Nist called, "The airships are in firing range!"

I could see Martin trying to get the attention of the patrol ship captains, but they were too busy maneuvering to pay him any attention! His ship too damaged to maneuver, Martin began a rapid, controlled descent. Surprised by Martin's move, the patrol ships' first few shots flew harmlessly over the stricken airship. If Martin could hold out for another few seconds, we'd be in among the patrol ships. We were no more than a hundred yards away from the battle when a ballista bolt hit the airship's envelope at just the right angle. Instead of punching straight in, it sliced along the edge of the envelope, ripping a gaping hole in it.

Gas poured through the rip and the envelope began to crumple!

# Chapter 17

"Nist, find the fastest way to get me to Martin's ship!" I cried, rushing to a coil of rope on the *Pauline's* deck. "Garrett, you've got to find a way to call off your patrol ships!"

"How?" Garrett demanded.

"Keep waving the flags. Shout. Jump up and down. Whatever it takes. Just get it done!" I said, tying one end of the rope to a docking cleat. "Nist, does the *Pauline* have enough lift to help Martin land safely?"

"Not at the rate he's losing gas," Nist replied, "but if we can get the patrol ships to stop shooting and help, I think we can do it."

"Then do whatever you have to do to make sure those patrol ships see Garrett!"

Nist grinned and began making course corrections. Seconds later, Nist squeezed the *Pauline* through the narrow gap between two of the patrol ships. With the *Pauline* steaming just feet from both patrol ships, Garrett—waving, jumping, and shouting—finally got the attention of the crews. Those two airships broke off their attacks as Nist dove toward Martin's flailing ship.

The third patrol ship finally spotted the *Pauline* and, more important, Garrett in the bow. The ship broke off its attack, too, leaving a clear path to Martin's airship.

"With the envelope flapping around, this is as close as I can get," Nist called to me a few seconds later.

We were twenty feet above the deck of Martin's ship and ten feet from its railing. It was farther than I'd have preferred, but I clutched the rope and took a running jump from the rail. Eight hundred feet of empty space yawned beneath me, then I crashed onto the deck of the stricken airship. Crewmen took the rope from me and rushed to tie it to an envelope mooring cleat.

Through all the commotion, I could hear Garrett shouting orders to his patrol ships, instructing them to render all aid to Martin's airship. I hoped they had some kind of procedure for aiding damaged ships, perhaps something similar to what I had done?

Half a minute later, I had my answer. Patrol ship crewmen began jumping to the deck, each holding the end of a rope. Lines were tied off and our descent began to slow. It finally stopped about a hundred feet from the ground.

Martin was kept busy directing the three patrol ships, the *Pauline*, and his own crew during the short flight to Pingor. Only when his ship was docked, did Martin come talk to me.

"I've got bad news, David," he said. "Not only is Callan right about Windslow being behind these kidnappings, I discovered he's not working alone."

"Who's working with him?" I asked, certain I knew the answer already.

Martin grimaced. "Raoul."

# Chapter 18

Before I could ask Martin for more information, the voice of Tristan Agrilla, well known as the Desert Doctor for his work among the southern desert tribes, rose from below deck.

"Martin! I need stretchers and stretcher bearers for the wounded." Climbing onto the main deck, Tristan's eyes focused on me for the first time. "Good to see you, lad! Could you please nip off and arrange a room for my patients?"

"How many have you got?"

"Too many! Twenty-two," Tristan replied. "None of them are very serious, though, so there's no need for an operating theater."

"I hear and obey, Mighty Healer!" I sketched a bow.

"Bah! You sound just like that scamp, Nist," Tristan replied. "Begone, boy!"

"Once the wounded are taken care of, you'll need to tell us what happened," I said to Martin, then dodged through the crowd to find Garrett.

Moments later, a line of stretchers was headed into Garrett's palace. Callan and I watched them pass, our worst fears ameliorated when Milo walked off the airship. His head was bandaged but his stride was steady. Milo gave us a smile which took on a strained quality when Callan pulled him aside and started checking him over.

"I'm fine, Cal— um, Your Highness," Milo protested. "You know Tristan would have me on a stretcher if I'd taken more than a bump on the head!"

"Just stand still and let her satisfy herself, Milo," I said. "It'll be easier for us all in the long run."

Callan had just finished giving Milo the once-over when Martin joined us. The four of us went to join Lord Garrett in his sitting room.

Garrett was busy reuniting with his family, one arm around Michelle's waist and the other holding Ann. Ellen was hugging one of

Garrett's legs, a big smile on her face. Brolan stood nearby, looking like he wanted to join in the hugging if only no one was watching.

"Now that I've had a chance to think about what's been happening," Garrett said, "what on earth do you think you're doing, Callie?"

"What do you mean, Uncle?"

"I understand why you engaged this ex-raider," Garrett pointed at Martin, "to fight the trog army, but the Royal Navy is no longer scattered to all points of the compass searching for you. So why isn't the capital fleet escorting you?"

"Ask Brolan," Callan replied. "He figured it out."

"Did he?" Garrett looked at his son. "Well, my boy?"

Brolan bit his lip and then blurted, "Because the admirals would still be making plans and keeping Callie under guard and the king and queen would be dead before the navy could find them!"

"I think you do our naval commanders a disservice," Garrett said, "though I suppose there is some truth to your reasoning."

"But?" Callan asked.

"But by now the navy is bound to be mobilized and starting another search for you, Callie. So your objections to dealing with the navy are no longer valid," Garrett responded. "Now it's time for you to return to the capital and let the navy handle this matter. If you apologize for the insult to the navy brass, I can persuade the admirals to chalk all of this up to the impetuousness of youth. No lasting harm need come of it."

"No lasting harm? The navy excels at many things, Uncle, but subtlety is not one of them," Callan said. "Windslow would see the navy coming from miles away. He'd have plenty of time to kill my parents and make good his escape before the navy even knew where Windslow was hiding."

"That's another thing," Garrett said. "Your only evidence of Windslow's involvement is the confession of a dying assassin! What if he was lying?"

"He wasn't lying, Lord Garrett," Martin said. "The damage to my ship occurred when we were attacked by Ardhan Windslow and Prince Raoul!"

# Chapter 19

"Remember the airship I was waiting for yesterday?" Bane asked. "Apparently Windslow and Raoul convinced—or bought, more likely—the loyalty of the ship's captain. I expect it happened sometime after I worked with the captain in Faroon. He was probably already working for them when I put the word out last night that I was hiring ships."

"A raider who sells out to the highest bidder?" Garrett sneered. "I'm shocked at his disloyalty!"

"Perhaps he simply took after the sterling examples of loyalty shown by some of your royal commanders!" Martin shot back. "There's the example of the western squadron captains thirty years ago, handsomely paid to sit idle and watch while a Tartegian fleet sailed across the border to attack. Or raiders could emulate Windslow, himself. How much does one have to pay the captain of the Royal Guard to mastermind a plot to kidnap a four year old princess?"

"Stop it, both of you!" Callan commanded. "Uncle, you will stifle your opinions and work with Martin. If you cannot do that, I'll take my leave of you right now and make do without the benefit of your advice."

Callan glared until Garrett nodded.

"As for you, Martin," she whirled to face him, "despite your obvious change of heart and your heroics at Faroon, you were a raider for fifteen years. It's going to take time to convince people you've changed. Learn to deal with it!"

"As you command, Highness," Martin said, flourishing a bow which was, for once, devoid of irony.

"Good. Continue with your report, Martin."

"As I said, I was waiting for one more airship, the *Kestrel*, before heading north to coordinate the search. When he arrived, Captain

Stubb and a few members of his crew came aboard for their briefing. Once we were below decks, the crew of the *Kestrel* swarmed aboard and had my men at sword point before they even realized what was happening," Martin said. "That's when Windslow and Raoul showed themselves. They wanted to know where they could find you. Stubb incidentally, wanted to take all the valuables we had onboard."

"Wait," Callan said. "They knew I hadn't been kidnapped?"

"They suspected it," Martin said. "I tried to lead them astray, Your Highness, telling them I had been hired by David to find you."

"Didn't they wonder why I wasn't with you?" I asked.

"Indeed. Alas, you were severely wounded defending Her Highness," Martin said. "You sent your trusted page, Milo, to me with instructions to find your wife."

"And they believed you agreed to help out of the goodness of your heart?" Garrett interjected.

"No, they believed I agreed to help because Princess Callan is my one and only patron among Mordanian royalty," Martin said. "No offense, David, but Raoul seems to think your good will is of no consequence without Callan."

"In that respect," Garrett said, "they are sadly mistaken."

Callan rewarded Garrett with a smile before nodding to Martin to continue.

"I told Stubb where to find our valuables and told my men to cooperate. Stubb's crew didn't appear eager to put us to the sword and I began to hope we were going to get out of the situation without a fight," Martin continued. "That's when Milo came up on deck. Tristan had sent him to see what was going on. I guess seeing Milo reminded Raoul of everything that happened in Faroon. Anyway, when Raoul spotted Milo, he lost all of his composure! Raoul drew his sword and attacked Milo!"

# Chapter 20

Garrett looked at Milo. "Raoul is a grown man. The lad can't be any older than Brolan."

"I'm fourteen!" Milo said, with the vehemence of a teenager accused of being younger than his true age

"Even so, it's still not very noble of Raoul to attack such a young lad," Garrett growled.

"As David has observed in the past, Raoul isn't particularly noble. Besides, 'tried to attack' is a much more accurate description of events," Martin said. "Raoul's leg buckled before he could reach Milo. I'd say that stab wound you gave him still hasn't fully healed, Your Highness.

"While Raoul struggled back to his feet, Milo darted below deck. Once he was on his feet, Raoul hobbled after him. With all the attention on Raoul, I elbowed Stubb in the stomach and ran after the prince," Martin said. "Raoul chased Milo into the surgery, hitting Milo on the head with the pommel of his sword. Tristan stepped between Raoul and the boy then tried to talk sense into Raoul. As most of you know, that's a waste of time, words, and breath. Raoul looked as if he was about to attack Tristan when I tackled Raoul from behind.

"I put a dagger at Raoul's throat just as Windslow and Stubb reached the door. They were backed by a couple of crossbowmen, so we had a bit of a stand off. Raoul makes a good bargaining chip— that's the one thing he's proven to be good for—and it's apparent Windslow doesn't want to risk upsetting the Tartegian royal house," Martin continued. "I ordered Stubb to pull his men back to his ship and to take Windslow with him. I promised Windslow I'd release Raoul once they were off my ship. In return, Windslow promised to leave in peace once they had Raoul. I kept my part of the bargain. Stubb, encouraged by Raoul, broke their part and attacked after our airships separated.

"My ship and crew weren't prepared for battle, so I took a page from your playbook, David. I Boosted and jumped across to Stubb's ship." Martin smiled, "You know, it's rather fun to be the dashing hero every now and then—even if there isn't a beautiful princess to rescue! I ran Stubb through before he could draw his sword—not very sporting of me, Lord Garrett, but Stubb *did* break his word! I slashed two crossbowmen who were taking aim at my crew and then had a clear run at Raoul.

"Raoul, meanwhile, had a clear run below deck. He took off as fast as he could hobble. I chased the coward into the captain's cabin and was ready to kill him right there. I thought I might get a medal from the Tartegians for taking care of their embarrassing Spare Prince. But I'd forgotten about Windslow. He followed me into the cabin, hit me on the head with a belaying pin, then shoved me over the railing of the captain's balcony!"

# Chapter 21

"The only thing that saved me from a very long fall was the flagpole for the Beloren flag Stubb flies from the stern of the *Kestrel*," Martin said. "Since I was still Boosting, I was able to catch the flagpole, swing around it, and pop back up onto the balcony. Windslow was just looking over the rail to watch me fall, so I plowed into him, knocking him backwards into Raoul. The two of them crashed to the deck and were just lying there helpless. I would have taken the opportunity to finish them off except a bunch of Stubb's crewmen piled into the cabin.

"Even Boosted, those were odds I just didn't like. I jumped from the balcony to the railing above and pulled myself onto the main deck. During the confusion, my ship had separated from the *Kestrel* and pulled away. They were circling nearby, waiting for me. The *Kestrel's* port ballista crew was watching my ship, just waiting for a chance to fire on it. I charged into them and knocked two of the crew overboard. That was too much for the remaining two crewman and they ran. I spun the ballista around to aim at the *Kestrel's* port engine and fired, blowing away the propeller. Then I took a running jump to my ship.

"The second I landed on the deck, the helmsman swung away from the *Kestrel* and we made a run for it. Despite the confusion on board, Stubb's crew managed to get off one good ballista shot. It nearly destroyed our steam engine. With Stubb wounded and the airship down to a single engine, the crew of the *Kestrel* didn't press the attack." Martin wrapped up, "We made what repairs we could then limped here for full repairs to the engine. And, thanks to the fine welcome we received, my ship also needs repair to its envelope!"

"Don't go there, Martin!" Callan warned.

Martin raised his hands in acquiescence, then said, "There is one more, rather important bit to the story. I think I know where Stubb is taking Raoul and Windslow. Unless I miss my guess, it's to wherever they're holding the king and queen."

"What makes you think that?" I asked.

"Stubb had a navigation chart laid out on the table in his cabin," Martin replied. "I only got a brief glance at it, but instructed my implant to record the image. If Lord Garrett has charts for the mountains northwest of here, I think I can show you where they're going."

Moments later, Martin selected a chart from those Garrett had ordered brought to us. Martin's finger pointed into the mountains. "Here. Stubb's chart had a mark right here."

Garrett leaned closer, "Of course! I can't believe it didn't occur to me!"

"*What* didn't occur to you, Uncle?" Callan asked.

"They're headed to the Aerie, a long-abandoned mountain fortress," Garrett said. "That's got to be where Windslow is holding the king and queen!"

# Chapter 22

"I admit it's compelling evidence and agree it's the first place we should check," I said, "but why would Windslow use any place on Mordanian soil, much less an old Mordanian fort?"

"The Aerie was Windslow's first post after he joined the military," Garrett said. "The fortress was built centuries ago to guard the only mountain pass between Tarteg and Mordan. The Tartegians have a similar fort at the other end of the pass. When airships came along, the fortress became obsolete. Who needs a mountain pass when you can just fly over the mountains? It was kept manned out of force of habit until my father closed the place. I was quite young when it was abandoned, but my personal guard told me all about the place."

"Was Windslow your personal guard?" Callan asked.

Garrett nodded. "The Aerie has been abandoned for forty years, it's hard to reach without an airship, and well fortified. It would be perfect for hiding royal hostages. If you'd had this information last night, Callie, you could have gotten there long before Windslow and Raoul. There's no chance of that, now."

"That's not necessarily true," Martin said. "They'll have to repair the port engine or limp along at half speed. Either way, a small, fast ship like the *Pauline* might get there before them, if it could make the entire run at full speed."

When I explained the situation to Tristan, he readily agreed to let us borrow his airship again. "You know Nist and the *Pauline* are available any time you need them. But you must take me along, too. Their Majesties may need medical care, especially if Windslow's men have been treating them roughly!"

I agreed, adding Tristan to our team of Nist, Martin, five of Garrett's men, and me. Garrett wanted to volunteer as well but Callan refused.

"You must go to Morda and keep the kingdom running smoothly," she said. "Someone from the family has got to sit on the throne and I won't be of legal age for another three months. There's no other choice—it's got to be you!"

"Callie, you don't understand how quickly a hostage's perception of reality can be subverted," he protested. "Hunger, thirst, and sleep deprivation can take a toll very quickly. If Windslow is also using drugs, which wouldn't surprise me, your parents may have a badly distorted memory of the last few months. They'll need to see a face they've known for years or they may not trust their rescuers. You need someone in the rescue party your parents will trust instinctively!"

"I know, Uncle," Callan said. "That's why I'm going with them!"

# Chapter 23

"You're going to do *what*?" Martin asked.

"My wife says she's going with us on the rescue mission," I said.

"And you don't have anything to say about that?" he asked.

"I must admit I share Bane's curiosity," Garret said.

Callan crossed her arms, "Choose your next words with care, darling."

"Garrett, you have already raised an excellent point. A familiar face may be necessary to get through to Callan's parents. Callan, you have raised the excellent point that someone must take the throne. Legally, that person must be Garrett. That means Callan should be the one to come with us," I said. Turning to Callan, I added, "But when we are inside that fortress, you have *got* to follow my orders. If you don't do that you could get someone killed."

"I understand," Callan said.

"Good, so you won't mind swearing to do as you're told?" I asked.

"Swear, David?" Callan's voice went flat.

"Callan, would you accept a man into your service if he said he'd guard you with his life but wouldn't swear an oath to that effect?" I asked. "It isn't a perfect analogy, but I'm trying to impress on you just how serious I am about this."

Callan shook her head and sighed. "On my honor as a princess of Mordan and heir to the throne, I swear to obey your orders on this rescue mission."

"If I hadn't seen it with my own eyes, I wouldn't believe it." Garrett turned to Callan. "Who are you and what have you done with my willful niece?"

"If she has enough close brushes with death, Uncle, even a willful niece can change," Callan said.

I wrapped my arms around Callan and kissed her. "Thank you, my dear. Your husband and the captain of your guard both appreciate your understanding. Now, let's gather supplies and get going."

It didn't take us long to get ready. Garrett placed the five-man squad he was sending with us under my command and the squad ensured the *Pauline* was well supplied. Light-weight camouflage netting was spread over the little ship's gas envelope, making it more difficult to spot from above.

As the mooring lines were cast off, Garrett said, "Bring her back safely to us, David."

"Count on it," I replied. "I've sworn an oath, too, after all!"

Then the *Pauline* was free and rising rapidly into the late morning sky. Nist flew faster than I would have thought possible for the little ship. The main reason Nist could fly so fast was because the five man squad took shifts feeding the fire, keeping the boiler pressure up. Martin handled navigation, using wind charts to plot the fastest course. He was able to direct our course so we picked up a tail wind, adding to our speed.

Having nothing to contribute to the operation of the airship, Tristan, Callan, and I spent the time studying an old floor plan for the Aerie. It was something Garrett had found in his library while our provisions were gathered. I could see three areas in the old fortress which seemed like secure places to keep prisoners. We'd have to hope for some sign to identify which of the three areas held the king and queen. Without something to point the way, we'd end up having to search through half of the fortress to find them! I doubted we'd have anywhere near that much time.

After a while, the plans to the fortress began to blur. I called for a break, suggesting we all get some rest while we could. It looked like we had a long night ahead of us.

Conversation waxed and waned as the little airship sped on toward the Aerie. One of the men served dinner as the sun sank below the horizon. We were lounging in the cabin, struggling against boredom, when Martin called us up on deck. Nist had brought the ship down to about fifty feet above tree level. A full moon bathed the night in soft, silver light.

Martin motioned us to the port rail and pointed off into the darkness. "Stubb's airship is over there, five or six miles off. We've caught up with them!"

# Chapter 24

I looked in the direction Martin was pointing and saw nothing but dark sky. Even with the light from the moon and the planetary ring, I was clueless as to the other airship's location. Since I don't have Martin's experience, I wasn't really surprised by that. Besides, a raider who couldn't spot a nearby airship in the dark probably ended up having a very short career.

"Do you think they can see us?" Callan asked the question on everyone's mind.

"I doubt it," Martin said. "We're flying at a much lower altitude than they are. Between the darkness and the camouflage netting over the envelope, the *Pauline* should blend into the background. I think we'll slip past them safely enough."

"It sounds like there's a 'but' in there somewhere," I said.

"There is. The *Kestrel* is making better time than I thought she would. We won't have anywhere near as much time to spare when we reach the Aerie as I had hoped," Martin said. Scratching his chin, he continued, "I'd guess we'll have an hour at most, and we'll spend a lot of that sneaking up to and into the fortress." He turned to me, "How goes the planning for sneaking into the Aerie?"

"It's going great, with one exception. I've identified three places that are secure enough to hold the king and queen," I said. "Unless you can offer some insight I haven't thought of, it could take us a lot more than one hour to find Callan's parents.

Martin thought for a moment, "Is one of the areas you found on the north face of the fortress?"

I had my implant recall the image of the map. "Good guess, Martin."

"It wasn't really a guess. Anyway, you should make your plans with the north facing area in mind," Martin said.

"Why do you think they'll be on that side, Martin?" Callan asked.

"The land north of the pass is nothing but mountains—and inhospitable ones at that. They can burn lights on that side without worrying about some farmer or a passing airship spotting the light and getting curious."

"This occurred to you because—and I'm just taking a wild guess, here—that's what you'd do," I said.

Martin just grinned in reply.

Callan and I went below and began planning our landing and entry into the Aerie from the north face of the fortress.

Three hours later, the Aerie came into view. It squatted atop the tallest mountain in the region, a huge, hulking fortification which commanded all that lay below it. It also looked like the perfect set for one of those horror vids my parents didn't want me watching when I was a kid. All it lacked was a howling wolf and dark clouds scudding across the face of the moon.

Nist kept our airship close to the ground and reduced speed, keeping our engine as quiet as possible. It wouldn't do for our engine noise to alert those within the Aerie! Slowly, Nist piloted us around the mountain.

When the north face swung into view, I said, "Callan, we'll have to tell your uncle that sometimes it very definitely helps to have a reformed raider on your side."

Light flickered from four of the north-facing windows!

# Chapter 25

It took Nist twenty minutes to complete his approach to the fortress, drifting in with the wind, only using the propellors to improve steering and maintain his heading. Despite the darkness and the crosswinds, Nist landed the *Pauline* in the exact spot Martin had selected when we were floating half a mile away from the fortress. Nist set the airship down on the wall in deep shadows, with a tower between us and the lit windows.

We climbed out onto the fortress wall as Martin issued instructions to Nist. "If Stubb's airship gets here before we're back, slip away as quietly as possible and go get help. If you have to sacrifice quiet to get away safely, do it. The map I gave you shows where all of my ships are and the search pattern they're following. Make for the closest pair of ships and send them back here. If you spot the Royal Navy along the way, send them instead."

Nist nodded his understanding and the rest of the team entered the tower. We descended the stairs within the tower until we reached the same level as the lighted windows. We didn't have to worry about the stone stairs creaking, but the ancient, rusted iron hinges on the doors were going to be a different matter. I'd been prepared to risk the squeal of rusted iron, but Tristan had a better idea.

Using chisels from the *Pauline*, we dug into the rotted wooden door and freed the door from its hinges. Three of the soldiers pulled the door from its frame and leaned it against the wall. It was quiet but took five precious minutes. I fervently hoped we wouldn't come across any more doors.

Slipping from hallway to hallway, we kept watch for patrolling guards. Whoever was in charge in the fortress wasn't expecting company, because we didn't see a single guard making the rounds.

Eight long minutes later, we got our first indication of life since we had spotted the lighted windows. The sound of metal banging on metal began echoing through the hallways. As the sound grew louder, we were able to discern a man's voice yelling over the sound.

"Wakey wakey, Your Majesty! I've got strict orders—no sleeping for you!"

I peered around a corner and saw a lantern burning at the far end of a long hallway. A lone man stood next to the lantern, banging an iron rod on the bars of a cell door. He cradled a cocked and loaded crossbow in his free arm. As I watched, he stopped hitting the bars in the door and peered into the cell.

"Yes, sit up! There's a good king! It's time for your medicine."

"What's happening?" a slurred voice asked. "W-where's my wife?"

Behind me, Callan gasped in dismay at that question.

"Oh, don't you worry none about the queen," the cell guard said, the smirk obvious from his tone. "She's gone to a fancy ball! The lads at the party will give 'er the time of 'er life!"

"David, we've got to hurry! I don't know what they're doing to my mother—" Callan's urgent whisper broke as she choked back a sob.

I scanned the approach to the cell. There were no closer cross corridors, so anyone approaching the guard would have to walk down a hundred feet of hallway in plain sight of the guard. He could sound the alarm long before we reached him. And, of course, anyone in the hallway would be an easy target for the crossbow.

I described what I saw to the others. "Boosted, Martin and I can dodge the crossbow bolts, but the guard could kill the king before we got close to him. Does anyone have any better ideas for approaching this guy?"

"I have one," Callan said, "but you're not going to like it."

That was an understatement. I *hated* it!

# Chapter 26

Martin, Callan, and I marched around the corner and into the long hallway. Martin walked ahead of Callan and me, his stride full of purpose and confidence. I held Callan's arm and walked a bit ahead of her, like I was pulling a reluctant prisoner along with me. Callan held her hands behind her back as if they were tied.

We were gambling that the guard would assume we were part of the team sent to kidnap Callan. There was a chance the man would recognize Martin or at least know him by his reputation, but Martin had that covered. If the guard got suspicious about Martin's change of allegiance, Martin was prepared to spin a story about gaining Callan's trust so he could aid in the kidnapping. With the airship carrying Windslow and Raoul bearing down on us, we had no time to come up with a plan I liked better—it was Callan's idea or a headlong charge.

When the guard noticed us, Martin raised his hand in greeting.

"We've got an extra guest for you!" he called.

"Bane? What are you doing here?" the guard called.

"Horst, good to see a familiar face!" Bane said. "After my contract ended, your employer made me an offer." He motioned back to Callan. "He wanted the full royal set, I guess."

A haggard face peered through the bars in the door next to the guard.

"Callie?" cried the king, his voice still slurred. "No, not my little girl, too!" The eyes shifted to Martin. "I know you! I'll—" the king grabbed the bar with both hands and tried to shake the door.

"You'll what? Take a firm tone with me?" Martin sneered. He turned to the guard, "Give my lad the key and walk with me for a moment. I've got new instructions."

Horst's eyes roamed appreciably over Callan's body as he handed me the keys. As he walked down the hall with Martin, Horst said, "It's gonna be fun having *her* around to party with!"

When Horst and Martin walked out of earshot, the king stared at me through heavy-lidded eyes and whispered, "Do I know you? I feel like I should." He shook his head as if trying to clear it. "No matter. You look like a smart young man. If you help us escape. I'll reward you handsomely!"

Unlocking the door, I whispered, "That's what I'm here to do, Your Majesty."

A thud sounded behind us. Martin had knocked out Horst.

Callan rushed into the cell and hugged her father. "Come on, Daddy, let's go find Mom!"

Martin returned and whispered, "We've got to hurry. Horst told me the other guards have vile plans for the queen!"

# Chapter 27

A fist hit Martin on the side of the head and he reeled against the wall. King Edwar followed it with a punch to Martin's stomach. As Martin doubled over, I caught the king's raised fist.

"The situation is not as you think, Your Majesty," I said.

"I know all I need to know," King Edwar snarled, the drug-induced stupor pushed aside by his rage.

Callan placed her hand on his arm, "No, you don't, Daddy, and we don't have time for explanations. Martin is here at great personal risk with no wish other than to help us!"

"Martin?" King Edwar asked. "You call this criminal scum by his given name?"

"I call him friend," Callan replied.

"What has happened to you, Callie?" her father asked.

"Nothing happened to me—which is why I know we can trust Martin." Callan took her father's hands and look into his eyes. "You've been beaten, deprived of sleep, drugged, and probably starved. I know what I'm doing and who I can trust!"

"But you're just a little girl!" my father-in-law said.

"No, Daddy, I'm a married woman who'll be twenty-one in a couple of months," Callan told him.

A puzzled look crossed Edwar's face. "Married?" He looked at me. "To you? Is that why you look familiar?"

"Yes, Edwar, it is," I said. "But right now we have to find the queen."

Martin straightened, wincing, "Horst told me the other men have gotten bored just sitting around. They're off gambling for first dibs on the queen!"

The color drained from the faces of Callan and her father.

"Do you have any idea where they've taken her?" I asked.

"Horst didn't want to have to listen—though more because he was on duty and unable to join in the fun than through any sense of decency—so he sent them to the far end of that side passage," Martin said, pointing at a passage back beyond where we'd first spotted Horst.

Callan started down the hallway toward the passage, the king on her heels.

"Stop, Callan," I said. "I'll get your mother. You and your father must go to the airship."

"I'm not going to run to safety while my mother is in danger!"

"Yes, you are," I said. "The kingdom comes first. That means ensuring the safety of the king and his heir!"

"But—"

"I'll rescue her, Callan."

"And I'll help," Martin said. "With two scouts—"

"No, Martin," I said. "You're the only person I can trust to fly off and leave the queen and me behind, if necessary. And that is exactly what you will do if the *Kestrel* arrives before I get back to you."

Martin nodded, "I'll keep them safe, David."

Callan kissed me. "Be careful, darling. I don't want to lose you or Mom!"

I nodded and took off down the side passage to find the queen!

# Chapter 28

As I neared the end of the passage, I heard raucous voices and rough laughter. Cries of excitement rose, followed by disappointed curses and one yell of triumph. The sounds all came from behind a closed door, one without a barred little window cut into it. The raised voices died down and the men launched into some kind of bantering discussion. I desperately wished I had some idea what was happening behind the door but I couldn't afford the time it would take to figure it out by listening through the door. Even if the queen wasn't in immediate danger—which didn't seem likely—the other airship could arrive at any time. I needed to get the queen to the *Pauline* so we could make good our escape.

Without giving myself the chance for second thoughts, I opened the door and strode into the room. I swept a critical gaze over the room. To my right was a large table around which sat five men. Dice were scattered across the table, along with several empty bottles of wine. The men were drinking from goblets and their eyes shone with excitement. The object of their attention stood to my left. A sixth man stood before the queen, looking her up and down. He wore a disturbing smile and was casually tossing a knife from hand to hand.

The queen's arms were spread wide, each wrist tied to an iron ring driven into the wall. Strips of cloth, which I suddenly realized were the queen's slashed clothing, were piled on the floor next to her. The queen was left wearing only her shift and the underclothes beneath it. Worst of all, my proud mother-in-law sagged forward, only kept up by the ropes around her wrists. Head hanging down, her dull eyes were open but were not focused on anything. Queen Elaina ignored all within the room. She didn't even look up as I entered the room.

The six men were so enthralled with their entertainment, they hadn't noticed me yet, either. That couldn't last long and I thought

61

my act would be more believable if I announced myself before they saw me.

"What is the meaning of this?" I demanded.

The heads of the five men at the table turned my way. The man standing before Queen Elaina gave a start before spinning to face me. To my considerable relief, the queen's head turned slowly toward me, as well.

Pointing at me with the knife, the man before the queen asked, "Who are you and what are you doing here?"

The men at the table rose from their seats and drew their swords.

It had been too much to hope the men would just accept that I had authority to match the tone of voice I'd used. Still, I did the only thing I could do at this point. I continued with my act.

"Our employer was afraid you cretins would do something stupid like this. You were under strict orders to keep the prisoners secure and unharmed!" That last bit was a complete guess, but it seemed like a reasonable one.

"Aw, we ain't harming 'er! We's jest havin' a bit of fun."

"You're not being paid to have fun, you idiot! It looks like our employer was wise to send me to insure the prisoner's safety." I held out my hand. "Give me that knife and get away from the queen!"

Keeping my left hand outstretched, I continued toward the man. He looked to one of the men at the table. I'd instilled doubt but the man wasn't ready to take orders from me yet.

"Your word don't cut it around here," one of the men at the table said. "Unless you got some written orders from the boss, you can just turn around and leave."

"Written orders? Just how stupid can you be?" I snarled. "And worse, just how stupid do you think our employer is? You don't honestly think he'd put anything about this in writing, do you?"

I'd kept walking during this exchange and was now within reach of the knife wielder. Drawing my sword, I slashed the man's forearm and the blade fell from his hand. He retreated away from me toward his friends at the table.

"The six of you stay here." I put all the derision I could muster—which was a lot, considering what I'd seen—into my voice. "I'll be back to deal with you after the queen is back in her cell and safe from the likes of you!"

At a signal from the apparent leader of this crew, a couple of men moved to block my way to the door.

"Tell you what, boy, what say you stop throwing around orders and answer a few questions for me?" the leader said. "Let's start with something easy—just who do you think you are?"

My bluster had gotten me farther than I had hoped it would, but the time for play acting was over.

"You want to know who I am?" I asked. "I am David Rice, prince consort and protector to Her Royal Highness, Princess Callan, heir to the throne of Mordan. I am the man who fought the trog leader in the city of Faroon and defeated him in hand-to-hand combat. I am the man who defeated the five assassins Ardhan Windslow sent to kill me and kidnap my wife. As far as you are concerned, I am death incarnate. Surrender now or die!"

# Chapter 29

My speech had very different effects on those who heard it.

Queen Elaina lifted her head and struggled to focus on my face. I hoped she could push through the drugs and sleep deprivation to recognize me. After King Edwar, though, I didn't have much hope.

I also hoped my reputation would lead the six men before me to surrender or, at the very least, back off and let us leave. It didn't. Instead, they laughed.

"Look, men, it's David the Pure—and the stories are true! I can feel his amazing powers of goodness driving the evil from my soul!" the leader said to his men. "We'd better do something before we all end up all noble-minded like Martin Bane. Do me a favor, men, and kill this idiot."

"I don't know, Nars," said the one whose arm I'd slashed. "You ever listened to them songs about Rice? He's s'pposed to be real good!"

Nars rolled his eyes. "You're not telling me you've started believing tavern songs, are you Jon?"

The four other men looked at their companion and laughed.

Jon smiled nervously, "Nah. I— I was jest funnin' with you, Nars."

Jon's concern had been my last hope that Queen Elaina and I could just walk away from this. As I had expected, there was only one way I was getting us both out of this alive.

*Boost!*

While the men were all distracted laughing at Jon, I charged. The move surprised all six of them. Instinctively, they all took defensive stances.

One of the men held his guard much too low. I didn't hesitate, attacking him with a slash aimed at his throat. Suddenly aware his guard was out of place, the man brought his blade up to block my swing. With Boost-enhanced speed, I changed direction and brought my attack down low. Before the man even registered what I had done, his sword passed harmlessly above my blade. I drove two feet of steel into his gut. Withdrawing my now-crimson blade, I threw the screaming man at the closest man to my right. The two of them went down in a tangle of limbs and blood. I kept moving.

Despite his song-induced concern about my reputation as a warrior, Jon jumped into cross blades with me. He made a surprisingly neat move and caught me in a bind. My survival depended on constant motion, so I rammed my knee into his groin. Jon's eyes rolled up and he doubled over, breaking the bind. As I spun past Jon, I cut his sword arm to the bone. With a metallic clatter, his sword fell to the floor. Jon dropped to his knees, cradling his arm and trying to stop the bleeding.

I had broken through the line of men, leaving two to my right and two to my left. I leapt onto the table and spun to face the room. Two men were already out of the fight. The other four looked stunned at the speed of it all. The smiles and the laughter were gone, replaced by smoldering anger. And festering fear.

"As you can see, the tavern songs didn't exaggerate my abilities," I said. "This is your last chance to surrender!"

"You're a quick one, boy, and good with that sword. I'll give you that," Nars said. "But you're not a real smart fighter. It seems to me you're way over here, standing on the table, and the queen is way over there, tied to the wall. Lon," Nars singled out one of his men, "go over to the queen. If this boy doesn't throw down his sword, kill her!"

# Chapter 30

The man closest to the queen—Lon, I assumed—raised his sword and stalked toward the queen. In the old adventure vids my father and I used to watch, there would have been a chandelier which I could use to swing over my enemies to protect my mother-in-law. I had a knife but it was simply a blade for cutting. It was too poorly balanced to throw effectively. So I threw the only other thing I had to hand.

My sword spun and flashed in the torchlight before burying itself between Lon's shoulder blades. His back arched and a hand scrabbled over his shoulder, trying to reach the sword. The other men gaped, their eyes locked on my blade. While they were distracted, I hopped from the table and grabbed one of the chairs.

Recovering his composure, Nars was just turning back toward me when I smashed the chair over his head. The chair splintered and the guard leader reeled under the blow. I delivered a spin-kick to Nars' head and he collapsed. I was left holding two pieces of the chair back. Armed with those sturdy clubs, I charged at the man nearest to me.

Eyes wide, the man slashed wildly at my neck. I blocked the swing with one piece of the chair then smashed the wrist of his sword arm with the other. Bones snapped and the man's sword fell from his hand. I cracked him across the head with one of my clubs. The man's eyes rolled back in his head and he dropped to the floor. I never stopped moving toward the queen.

The third man broke and ran toward the queen. There was no way I could get to her first, so I hurled one of the pieces of the chair at his head, then threw the second piece at his legs. He ducked and the first piece missed, but the second piece hit a shin, tripping him up. That slowed him down long enough for me to dash to Lon, who was still flailing and trying to reach the sword stuck in his back. I rammed the blade through him up to the hilt.

Putting my foot against Lon's back, I shoved him away and yanked my blade free. I spun to face the man I'd tripped up with the thrown chair pieces. He stopped his stumbling charge toward me, arms windmilling wildly. His eyes went wide in terror and he dropped his sword.

"I surrender!"

"Smart man," I said.

I clouted him over the head with my sword pommel. As he fell unconscious, I dropped Boost.

As I cut the queen free, she asked in a slightly slurred voice, "You said you were Callie's guard? You're not Rob!"

"Yes, Your Majesty, I'm Princess Callan's guard," I said. "And no, I'm not Rob. But let's discuss that later. Her Highness is not far from here. She's with her father. And we need to join them before a raider airship arrives!"

# Chapter 31

Rubbing her chafed wrists, the queen peered at my face through heavy-lidded eyes. "You look familiar. And you said you were a prince consort? I didn't catch your wife's name. Is she known to me?"

"I believe so, Your Majesty." I helped Queen Elaina step into her shoes and then, taking her by the arm, led her from the room. "But as I said before, we must hurry."

"Yes, there is a raider ship on the way." The queen came to a sudden halt. "It's not that raider Martin Bane, is it? He's taken my baby before, you know!"

"I do know, Your Majesty," I replied, struggling to keep my voice calm and soothing. "But the man I'm worried about is most definitely not Martin Bane!"

I started walking again, giving the queen little choice but to stumble after me.

Unable to maintain focus, Queen Elaina's attention wandered yet again. Her head swung back and forth as she watched the sword I held in my other hand. Despite the drugs, she proved quite capable of recognizing the blade. "Why do you carry Captain Vonsteader's sword, young man?"

I didn't have the time or the creativity to craft a believable story on the spur of the moment. "I'm afraid Rob lost his life defending Princess Callan. He gave me the sword before he died and ordered me to use it in defense of your daughter."

The queen bowed her head, "Poor Callie. She must be devastated."

Three months had passed since Rob's death, but Callan still mourned her long-time companion and guardian. "That she is, though she tries to hide it."

Queen Elaina came to a sudden stop yet again. "Wait a moment, young man! You said you were a prince consort *and* protector to a princess. And you say Rob ordered you to defend Callie."

I could almost see the wheels turning in the queen's mind as she struggled against the drugs to make connections. I most definitely did *not* want to discuss my marriage to Callan right now.

"Let's keep moving, Your Majesty," I said, once again nearly dragging Queen Elaina down the hallway. "Princess Callan will explain everything once we're aboard the airship!"

"That would mean *you* married Callie," Queen Elaina mused. Shaking her head, she continued. "But that can't be right. Callie is marrying Prince Rupor, isn't she?"

"That was the plan," I said, walking faster. "We've got to hurry, Your Majesty! Time is short and we don't want the airship to leave without us!"

Elaina continued to stumble along behind me and we moved more slowly than I'd have preferred, but at least we were moving. Soon, I could see the corridor where we'd first seen Horst, the cell guard. We were no more than thirty feet from the hallway when I heard voices.

Putting my finger to my lips in the hopes of keeping Elaina quiet, we stopped and listened. There could be no mistaking the voice.

"I thought you said there was a guard in this hallway?" Raoul said, his tone short and peremptory.

The queen's face lit up. "Why that's Raoul, Rupor's brother! He'll have a whole ship full of men with him. Those raiders you're so worried about are in for a rude surprise!"

"No, Your Majesty," I said, grasping for the only idea I could think of. "It's a raider trick to lure us out!"

"Pish and tosh! I'd recognize Raoul's voice anywhere." Queen Elaina waved my objections aside. Raising her voice, she called, "Raoul! We're down here!"

Boots clattered on stone as our enemies rushed toward us!

# Chapter 32

I was staging one heck of a rescue. Addled by drugs and sleep deprivation, the queen had asked all the wrong questions and, based on my answers, made all the wrong connections. She might not be suspicious of me yet, but Raoul would turn her against me if he had a chance to speak with her. I could only begin to imagine how she would react if I tried to convince her that Raoul wasn't the friend her memory told her he was. Unfortunately, I had to try to convince her of just that!

Light and shadows flickered on the wall at the intersection of the two hallways. The heavy tread of boots pounded closer to our passageway. Much as I wanted to explain the situation, I simply didn't have the time to do so. I had hoped I could get Queen Elaina to Callan and the king. Their presence would have calmed the queen. Rest and time would restore her memory and the queen would remember I was the good guy. Right now, we needed to run.

I lifted the queen and threw her over my shoulder. Or I tried to do that. The queen held her body rigid, refusing to bend over my shoulder. I couldn't outrun anyone with the queen throwing off my balance like that! It was time to improvise. I lifted the queen's legs, balancing her over my shoulder like a wooden board. It was still awkward, but at least I could run.

Realizing holding herself stiff hadn't slowed me down, the queen suddenly went limp. The sudden shift of weight threw me off balance again and I stumbled. As I fought to regain my footing, the queen beat and scratched at my back and began screaming, "Help me, Raoul! A raider has me!"

Our pursuers rounded the corner just in time to see me lurch into a side hall.

"There he is!" Raoul yelled. "Save the queen, men!"

70

Raoul didn't sound believable to me, but the queen kept shouting.

"Stop shouting, Your Majesty!" I said. "Raoul is not the friend you think he is!"

"Foolish man, do you really expect me to believe that? Raoul is the brother of my daughter's betrothed!"

"He wishes!" I said. "Look at our pursuers, Majesty. Do you see an older man with wild, gray hair?"

"Yes, I see him. What of it?"

"Look at him more closely. Don't you recognize him?"

"I can't—" The queen gasped, "Is that Windslow?"

"Yes, it is," I said. "That's extremely strange company the prince is keeping, don't you think?"

I came to a side passage, the first I'd seen in this hallway. Without hesitation, I turned into the hallway. I immediately saw that the hallway ended in a door, but it was too late to turn around.

"I don't know! It's so hard to think!" the queen moaned

"Then I suggest you trust me," I said. "I promise you Princess Callan does."

Raoul, Windslow and their men charged into the side passage as I reached the door. Hoping to find stairs, I turned the knob and pushed. Nothing happened. The door was stuck fast!

# Chapter 33

The queen hung limp over my shoulder, no longer beating and scratching my back. I hoped that meant she had decided to trust me. I was afraid it meant she had been overcome by the stress of her ordeal and the stress of seeing Windslow.

Seeing my struggles with the door, Raoul and his men slowed to a walk. "You can't escape, Rice. Return Her Majesty to me unharmed and I'll make sure you get a fair trial."

I had to give Raoul top marks for sticking to the script. If I had the opportunity, I would cut those marks into his forehead with my sword!

"Drop the play acting, Raoul. Her Majesty has already spotted Windslow and now knows you're not to be trusted," I said. "It wasn't very smart bringing him with you, but intelligence never was your strong suit. In truth, I'm still trying to figure out what your strong suit is."

"Do not try my patience, Rice!" Raoul cried, his eyes narrowing in anger. "Your fate hangs by a very narrow thread. Anger me further and I'll cut that thread without compunction!"

"Well, I'm impressed, Raoul. I didn't realize you knew such big words!" I said. "Or did you say 'without compunction' when 'without courage' is what you meant to say?"

Raoul's face went red and he sputtered incoherent curses. Entertaining as that was, it was time to make my getaway. While bantering with Raoul, I'd considered my options. There was but one option and in other circumstances it wouldn't have been an option at all. If the Terran Exploration Corps ever found me, I was going to be quite the case study on the effects of Boost on the human body. At least I'd only Boosted for a minute or so when dealing with thugs guarding the queen.

*Boost!*

I spun and kicked the door at the end of the hallway. The latch held firm, but the rusted hinges groaned and that side of the door moved an inch. Raoul shouted to his men to charge as I gave the door another kick. The hinges broke and the door pushed open a couple of feet. Releasing Boost, I ran through the door.

"After them! You stay with the men, Raoul," Windslow shouted at him. "I'll get back to the airship and take off! Aloft, I may be able to block their escape!"

Beyond the door, I found just what I needed—stairs going up. I kicked the door shut in the face of Raoul's charging men and then sprinted up the stairs. I hoped the next door I came to would open on the first try. Two flights up, the stairs ended at a landing with a door. The hinges squealed like dying animals but the door opened.

I charged through the door and onto the top of the fortress wall. It stretched out before me, bathed in silver moonlight. Silhouetted against the moon, I saw something which buoyed my spirits even as it doomed Queen Elaina and me. A dark shadow moved away from the Aerie—it was the *Pauline* flying away.

Callan and her father were safe—but the queen and I were trapped in the Aerie!

# Chapter 34

The queen stirred and attempted to straighten up. Perhaps the cold, fresh air was breaking through the drugs and fatigue affecting her mind.

"You can put me down, David," Queen Elaina said.

"You remember me, Your Majesty?"

"Yes, or at least some things about you," she replied. "I remember your name and know that I can trust you."

That would be more than enough for now, especially when I heard the door I'd kicked shut just a moment ago crash open.

"Can you run, Your Majesty?" I asked. "I am going to need to keep my sword arm free."

"Yes, I can," the queen answered. As I swung her to her feet, she continued, "You're more than Callie's bodyguard, aren't you, David?"

"I'm her husband," I said as I took her hand and began running along the wall toward the next tower.

"And Edwar and I approved?"

"Yes ma'am. You and His Majesty have been very kind and welcoming to me."

"Good for us," Elaina said, beginning to pant at the exertion. "That little airship you were watching—Callie and Edwar are aboard? I assume it was also our way out of this fortress?"

"It was, but only if we reached it before Windslow and Raoul arrived," I said. "If we didn't, my orders were for them to leave us behind."

"Why would you give such orders, David?"

Shouts erupted behind us as Raoul's men spotted us.

"A kingdom must have a monarch and an heir," I said, running faster and pulling Elaina with me. "That airship carries both."

"I can see why I approved of you, David. You're a very practical man," the queen said as we reached the door into the tower.

To my relief, the door opened easily and we ran inside the tower. To my consternation, there was no way to bar the door from the inside. Drawing my knife, I jammed it under the door. Perhaps it would slow down our pursuers for a few extra seconds.

The tower had stairs, but they only went up to the top of the tower. That was out of the question. We'd be trapped at the top of the tower and make easy targets for airborne crossbowmen. Even worse, there was no other door out the other side of the tower.

"I'm afraid this is where I must make my stand, Your Majesty," I said.

"After watching you fight, I have full confidence in you," the queen said.

I sighed. Boost was our only hope—and likely my death sentence. "You must run from the tower as soon as I clear a path for you."

"And what of you?" she asked.

"Chances are I'll be dead."

The tower door shook from a sharp blow. I raised my sword and prepared to defend my new family one last time.

# Chapter 35

The door rattled from another blow. On the other side of the door, Raoul exhorted his men to try harder.

"David, I'd rather not lose my son-in-law before I've had the chance to remember him." Elaina said. "Would you mind being a bit more practical and little less heroic?"

"Uh, sure," I replied.

"Good. Come over here with me." She backed up to the wall next to the door hinges. "When the door swings open, it will block us from view. We can hope the men will see the stairs and assume we climbed them. That will give us a chance to run out the door."

I joined her as the door shook again. "What happens if they don't take the bait? I mean, it is one of the oldest tricks in the book!"

"Either you'll get your chance to die heroically or, more likely, I'll choose to surrender," the queen said. "Whatever I decide, you will obey my commands."

I lifted my sword in salute. "As you say, Your Majesty."

Another blow struck the door. My poorly balanced knife was holding much better than I'd hoped, but now I needed the door to swing open. I wrenched the knife from under the door, standing up just ahead of the next blow. The door jamb broke and the door was flung open. We were hidden from sight by the door, but it threatened to smash into my face as well! I caught and held the door handle, saving my nose in the process.

Raoul's men charged into the tower and their footsteps continued toward the stairs. We waited for the men to reach the far wall before slipping around the door and out onto the fortress wall. I felt just like one of the heroes in the adventure vids from my childhood! Unfortunately, one of Raoul's men followed the same script and looked toward the door as we ran through it.

"Your Highness, they're behind us!" the man shouted as he set off after us.

And just like that the chase was on again, with Raoul and his men trailing us by no more than thirty feet. I pulled the queen along with one hand and sheathed my sword with the other. I could draw it again if need be, but expected I would need a free hand to open a door before I would need to swing my sword again.

Coming from the courtyard of the Aerie, I heard the roar of steam engines driving an airship into a climb. Windslow must have reach Stubb's airship and was bringing it to join the chase. Her Majesty and I had to get off of the wall soon. If we didn't, we would be easy targets for Stubb's airborne crossbowmen!

# Chapter 36

The roar of the airship's engines deepened and I could detect movement in the darkened castle courtyard. The *Kestrel* rose from the shadows and powered into the moonlight.

"You can't get away from us, Rice," Raoul called, as he chased Queen Elaina and me across the wall. "Our airship will cut you off before you reach the other tower. Even if it doesn't, our crossbowmen will cut you down!"

"Do you really want to be responsible for starting a war between Tarteg and Mordan?" I called back, picking up speed in the hopes of proving him wrong. "Callan's uncle, Lord Garrett, knows you are working with Windslow! If we don't return, you can count on Tarteg paying the price for your actions."

"Why would I care what happens to a country which turned its back on my mother and me?" Raoul shot back.

"What did you expect would happen after your role in Callan's kidnapping was exposed?" I asked over my shoulder. "You'd be welcomed back as the unconquoring wannabe hero?"

"I'm going to rip your heart out with my bare hands, Rice!" Rupor screamed over the engine noise from the approaching airship.

"Is it wise to taunt Raoul like that, David?" Queen Elaina asked between gasps for air.

"Most definitely. Raoul makes his worst mistakes when he lets his emotions get the better of him," I replied. I decided not to mention just how much fun it was, as well.

Screaming in wordless rage, Raoul put on an unexpected burst of speed and pulled away from his squad of men. The men sped up, trying to keep up with their enraged leader.

Unfortunately, the queen slowed down, unable to keep up the pace I'd been setting. Her chest heaved and her breath was ragged.

"I can't keep going," she gasped. "Leave me! Escape and return to Callan."

The *Kestrel* swung up over the castle wall, little more than a hundred feet behind us. The helmsman steadied the airship ten feet above the fortress wall. The massive vessel bore down on the two of us, already flying twice as fast as we could possibly hope to run. Windslow was perched at the bow of the ship, pointing at me with his sword and directing the *Kestrel's* crossbowmen.

Our eyes locked over the distance and a grin stretched over Windslow's face. "It's the end of the line, bodyguard. Prepare to die!"

# Chapter 37

I tensed, ready to risk Boosting again. I had kept my Boosts short so far today, but between the fight in the mine and the fight in the fortress, I was pushing my body harder than I had in months. Even Boosted I doubted I could block the two-dozen quarrels which would be flying at us shortly. I could, however, put my body between the crossbowmen and the queen. Windslow raised his arm. No doubt, dropping it would be the signal to fire.

"Stay behind me, Your Majesty!" I said, stepping in front of her. "I'll protect you as best I can."

Raoul and his men had stopped their pursuit, not wanting to put themselves in the line of fire. Windslow grinned, nodding in approval. Raoul's head swung between Windslow and me, his eyes wide in frenzied rage.

"Don't kill him, Windslow!" Raoul yelled. "Rice must die by my hand!"

"Don't be foolish, boy!" Windslow called back. "It doesn't matter how Rice dies—just that he ends up dead!"

Windslow raised his arm a bit higher—for added effect and drama, I suppose—and posed for just a second, his eyes locked on mine.

With a roar, the *Pauline* crested the outer wall and struck the bow of the larger airship. Windslow and his crossbowmen staggered as the deck heaved beneath their feet. Ragged twangs sounded as the crossbowmen's fingers twitched and they fired involuntarily. Unaimed quarrels flew in all directions. One quarrel pierced a crossbowman's leg. Another one of the quarrels slammed into the shoulder of one of Raoul's squad. The rest of the squad dove to the ground, leaving Raoul the only one of them standing.

Nist worked the *Pauline's* controls and flew straight along the wall toward us. In the little ship's wake the helmsman of the *Kestrel* fought to bring the larger airship back on course. I could see Martin and the soldiers standing at the rail, ready to toss ropes to us.

"Lovely to see you again, Raoul!" I shouted as the *Pauline* passed over his head. "As always, I've enjoyed watching your plan fail in such a spectacular fashion!"

Raoul broke into a run, waving his sword and shouting curses I couldn't hear over the *Pauline's* engines.

On the *Pauline*, Martin yelled, "Are you ready?"

"Yes!" I shouted, wrapping an arm around the queen. "Throw me a rope!"

I saw a subtle change in Martin and his movements became more fluid and graceful. He was Boosting to make his throw more accurate!

"Hold on tightly, Your Majesty," I said, pulling the queen close against me with one arm. Her arms wrapped around me, careful not to interfere with my free arm.

Martin threw the rope and it landed right in my free hand. I grabbed hold of the rope and we were yanked into the air.

The next tower on the wall was less than a hundred feet ahead of the airship. Having little choice, Nist spun the wheel and steered the *Pauline* over the edge of the Aerie's walls. A two-thousand-foot drop yawned beneath us as Martin and the soldiers hauled on the rope. Queen Elaina buried her head against my chest, unable to bear to watch as we were pulled to the ship. The few seconds we dangled in the air seemed unending, but end they did.

Hands caught us as we reached the airship and the two of us were pulled to the safety of the deck. Right after we reached the deck, a crossbow quarrel struck the airship. Looking back, I saw Raoul climbing on board the *Kestrel* with Windslow. Ropes had been thrown to him and his squad on the wall.

Raoul, rage still written on his face, was giving chase!

# Chapter 38

The air hummed as another quarrel flew past me, driving deep into the deck with a resounding thunk. Several other quarrels missed the airship entirely, their passage marked by sound alone.

"Your Majesties, Callan," I said, "you need to get into the cabin, now! That goes for you too, Tristan."

Tristan shepherded Callan and her parents below deck and out of immediate danger from the crossbow fire.

"Everyone find something to hold onto!" Nist yelled. "I'm going into a steep dive."

"Good idea, Nist," I said. "Raoul has a lot more men and firepower than we do. What can Martin and I do to help?"

"I'm stuck at the wheel and can't dodge incoming shots. Can you put up something to block them, instead?"

Nist hadn't finished talking before Martin and the soldiers began piling supply crates up behind Nist. The wall was only a few feet high when one of the soldiers cried out as a quarrel buried itself in his chest.

"Carry that man below deck," I told two of the soldiers. "If Tristan needs your help to setup a surgery, stay below and help him."

The two soldiers nodded and ran to carry their wounded comrade to our doctor.

Then the deck tilted under us as Nist put the *Pauline* into a dive. The engines roared and the little airship began picking up speed. Caught by surprise, the *Kestrel* was slow to respond to Nist's maneuvers. We began to pull away from the larger airship, but the other ship's altitude meant they could continue firing down on us. The next two volleys missed us entirely, but by then the *Kestrel's* helmsman had pointed the ship's nose down. We had gained a few hundred feet, but Raoul and Windslow were back on our tail!

"They're following us, Nist!" I yelled over the whistling wind and the roaring engines. "Have you got any idea how to get out of this?"

"If we can get the pressure up in the boiler, we can just outrun them!" Nist said. "We used up a lot of pressure coming up to ramming speed back at the wall. And until now, everyone has been busy pulling you and Her Majesty safely onboard the *Pauline!*"

"Martin—" I began.

"I'll deliver the orders to the men below, David!" Martin called as he ran toward the cabin door.

A crossbow quarrel hit one of the boxes piled up behind Nist. Another quarrel clanged off of a brass fitting. It looked like Raoul's men were getting a feel for the range and elevation.

I went back to dragging crates close to the wall we were building to protect Nist. The crates were heavy. I'd definitely need Martin's help to add any of them to the stack. And just like that, Martin returned and we lifted the crate together, adding it to the wall protecting Nist.

Meanwhile, Raoul's crossbowmen were getting organized, firing in rotation and, now that they were getting the range, keeping us under a near constant barrage of crossbow quarrels.

Martin and I rushed to finish building a wall for Nist before Raoul's crossbowmen really got the range figured out. Then it was too late. The next volley rained down on us and one of the quarrels struck the crate between the splayed fingers of my left hand. In a rush, Martin and I added the crate to the stack then leapt over the wall of crates, seeking shelter from the crossbowmen.

Midway through our leap, Martin grunted in pain. When we landed on the deck, I glanced at Martin, who was still lying on top of the crates. A quarrel had buried itself in his shoulder. I pulled him down behind the crate wall, propped him against it, and started to examine his shoulder. With a sigh, Nist collapsed next to us. Despite the wall we had built, a quarrel stuck out from between his shoulder blades.

With no one to man the controls, the *Pauline* leveled off and slowed down. Raoul's airship, still under the control of her helmsman and emulating the bird of prey it was named for, dove toward us from above!

# Chapter 39

"Do something, David!" Martin gasped. "You need to find a way to keep them off of us for a few minutes while the boiler pressure comes up."

Another rain of crossbow quarrels fell around us. If I stood in at the wheel for any length of time, I was sure to be shot. I thought I might be able to pilot the airship while crouching low enough that the wall of crates would protect me. It was worth trying, at least!

I scurried to the airship's controls, grabbed the wheel with one hand and the aileron controls with the other. Keeping my head down, I worked the ailerons and put the *Pauline* back into a dive. I was sure we were at least a thousand feet from the ground, but I couldn't both keep my head down and see what was ahead. At some point, I'd have to stand up to look and risk ending up like Nist.

"Martin, what are the chances you can get Nist down to Tristan?"

"Absolutely none," Martin said through gritted teeth.

"I didn't think so," I said. "Different question—can *you* get below deck and send someone back for Nist?"

"Yeah, I can do that," Martin said. "What about you?"

"I'll stay here, pilot the ship, and hope we get out of crossbow range before we crash into a mountain."

"Aren't you the cheery one?" Martin asked.

Another volley of crossbow quarrels hit the deck and the crates piled up behind us. The sound of the last quarrel striking wood hadn't faded when Martin jumped to his feet and ran for the cabin door. He threw the door open and dove through a split second before the next volley clattered on the deck where Martin had been standing.

Right after the next volley, two of Garrett's soldiers dashed through the door and up to join me on the deck.

As they carefully lifted Nist between them, one of the men asked, "What can we do to help you, sir?"

"Go back to stoking the fire," I said. "Outrunning the other airship is our best chance of survival."

"Yes, sir!" the soldier said, waiting for the next volley to pass. When it did, the two soldiers dashed off with Nist. Despite their burden, they were through the cabin door and safely under cover before Raoul's men could take any further shots.

At the same time, I risked popping up from concealment to see what was ahead. It was a good thing I did! The side of a mountain was no more than two hundred feet ahead of us!

# Chapter 40

I spun the wheel, changing our course away from the looming mountain, and worked the ailerons to level off. As a result of Nist's piloting, we had been at long range for the crossbows. And if Nist were piloting the ship right now, we'd be farther ahead than we were and probably pulling away from the other airship as well. But I was piloting and I just wasn't as skilled as Nist. In avoiding the mountain and leveling off, I overworked the ailerons and the *Pauline* nosed up twenty degrees. Too much hard won speed bled off before I could level off again. I looked over my shoulder to find the *Kestrel* looming large and closing.

Another volley of crossbow quarrels clattered all around me. Raoul certainly had his men firing without pause. Maybe we'd get lucky and they'd run out of quarrels before they hit anyone else. It wasn't likely, but hoping for that seemed the most useful thing I could think of to do.

Light spilled onto the deck as the cabin door opened then vanished as the door shut again. Light footsteps pattered across the deck. Even before she threw herself behind the makeshift barrier, I knew Callan had joined me on deck!

"What are you doing out here, Callan? You should stay below where it's safe!"

"Safe from what? If we don't find a way to get the *Kestrel* off our tail, Raoul and Windslow are going to catch all of us," Callan said. "Better I take a risk to help you than stay below and wait for us to get captured—or killed!"

I couldn't find fault with her argument, but that doesn't mean I had to like it.

"Well, darling," Callan asked, "what's the plan?"

"I'm trying to think of one, dear," I responded. "And in case you're wondering, my masculine pride won't be bruised in the least if you have any suggestions to offer!"

"Until the boiler pressure builds, we can't outrun them," Callan mused, "so maybe you should give up on speed and rely on maneuverability."

It was worth a try! I spun the wheel hard to starboard and our airship turned quickly to its new heading, off at right angles from the old course. We lost speed and the *Kestrel* drew closer, but now we were on a completely different heading than they were! We heard a volley of quarrels pass behind us as the crossbowmen lost their aim.

Within seconds of our course change, the *Kestrel's* helmsman was bringing the big ship around to our course. Worse, I had picked a course which allowed the bigger ship's crew to bring the starboard ballista to bear on the *Pauline*! With a deep thrum of springing wood and rope, a massive bolt was hurled across nearly two hundred feet. With a horrific crash, the bolt smashed into our airship's rudder! The tension went out of the wheel as the cables running to the rudder were snapped.

The *Pauline* still flew, but I no longer had control over the airship!

# Chapter 41

"I wish I hadn't made the suggestion to try to out maneuver them," Callan said in a small voice.

"It wasn't the suggestion, Callan, it was the course I chose," I said. "But let's worry about recriminations after we figure out what to do next!"

I looked about the moonlit deck for something—anything—I could use to defend us from the rapidly closing *Kestrel*. Nothing I saw sparked an idea.

*Spark!* That was it!

"Callan," I said, "can you light a lantern with a flint and tinder?"

"Of course. That was one of the skills Rob made sure I learned!" Callan replied. "But won't a lit lantern make it easier for the crossbowmen to hit us?"

The latest volley struck all around us. As soon as the last quarrel had hit, I dashed from behind our makeshift cover, grabbed the *Pauline's* stern lantern, and then snagged a mooring line as I dove back behind cover. Three quarrels struck where I'd been just a second ago.

"They don't seem to be having any trouble hitting us in the dark," I said. "So please light this!"

"Are you sure?" Callan asked.

"Trust me!"

Striking the flint, Callan said, "Always!"

Holding the mooring line, I jumped off the airship's port side and swung around toward the bow. The *Pauline* blocked me from the sight of Raoul's men as I swung forward, though I think I'd have been a tough target to hit even without the cover. Landing at the bow, I snatched the lantern hanging there and was swinging back to the stern before Raoul's men even knew where I was.

The stern lantern was burning brightly when I ducked behind the crates again.

"Nice work, my dear!" I said, swapping lanterns. "Light this one while I'm gone."

"Gone where?" Callan asked.

Perhaps I should have answered her, but I was in too much of a hurry. The latest volley of quarrels struck the ship and I charged out from behind the makeshift wall and toward the stern. By now, the pursuing airship loomed no more than eighty feet behind us.

At the rail, I flung the lantern at the *Kestrel*. It arched into the night as I ran back for the second lantern. Shouts erupted behind me as I dove back behind the crates. Once again, Callan had the lantern burning brightly. I took the second lantern and ran back to the stern. The first lantern had hit on the bow of the *Kestrel*. The dry wood of the airship's hull had caught fire quickly. The flames were spreading fast as the crew tried to figure out how to fight a fire they couldn't reach. Windslow, Raoul, and a man I assumed was Stubb were at the bow, directing the efforts to quell the blaze.

I aimed for the knot of crewmen on deck, hoping to hamper their efforts to put out the fire. The second lantern struck Windslow full on the chest and shattered! Burning oil splashed all over Windslow and he was engulfed in flames. Screaming in agony and fear, Windslow flailed at all around him. Rope, wood, and crewmen's clothing caught fire and panic flashed through the crew.

Raoul cast one baleful look toward the *Pauline* before doing the only thing he possibly could do about Windslow. Lifting a foot, Raoul kicked Windslow in the back. The fiery form toppled over the *Kestrel's* railing and dropped, flaming and flailing, a thousand feet to the valley below.

Ardhan Windslow would never again threaten the royal family of Mordan!

# Chapter 42

Working the ailerons allowed me to steer the *Pauline* somewhat. Keeping her speed low, I moved us a couple of hundred yards away from the dying *Kestrel.*

Screams floated across the distance from the flaming airship, along with the twang of taut lines as they weakened and snapped. The airship began dropping as the crew raced to land the ship before they burned to death or lost too many support lines, allowing the hull to break free from the gas envelope and plummet to the ground.

Now that we were free from pursuit and out of range of the other airship's weapons, I released the controls and ran to the cabin. Callan was right behind me. Tristan was tending to the soldier with a leg wound, aided by Queen Elaina. Nist was resting on his stomach, eyes shut and breathing evenly. Martin leaned against the wall, the crossbow quarrel still stuck in his shoulder, drinking brandy and chatting with King Edwar. A blanket covered the body of the guard who had been hit in the chest.

Spotting us, Martin called out, "Tristan says Nist will survive. Further, though my wound is dire indeed, the good doctor sent me to sit in the corner without even giving me a bottle of brandy!"

"And yet you have somehow managed to get your hands on a bottle," I noted.

"His Majesty was kind enough to fetch one for me," Martin said. "You'll be pleased to know I've been helping him and Her Majesty sort through their memories and to circumvent the effects of the drugs. They seem to recall thinking rather highly of you, David."

"Well I should hope so!" Callan said, taking my arm. "It's a little late for second thoughts!"

"I assume your presence down here means we are safe from pursuit?" King Edwar asked.

I nodded and then Callan launched into an explanation of what had happened to the *Kestrel*.

With no threats looming, I was suddenly exhausted. I laid down and Callan cradled my head in her lap. In seconds, I was asleep.

Daylight was streaming in the portholes when I awoke. Shouts rang all around us and I started to jump up to investigate. Smiling, Callan bent over and kissed me so soundly I knew we must be safe.

"A pair of Martin's ships found us just before dawn," she said. "They've almost finished repairing the rudder. We'll be underway and heading home shortly."

"Oh, well, if there's no need for a gallant hero, I'll just stay here with you," I said. "Assuming you aren't getting tired of cradling my head."

"I never will." Callan bent over and kissed me again.

Ardhan Windslow was dead and there was a lot of work waiting for us back at the palace. But my family and friends were safe. I put everything else out of my mind and went back to kissing the most beautiful woman on eight planets. As always, time went away and all was right in my world!

# PART 2

# SCOUT'S OATH

# Prelude

*David is Seven*

"It took me ten minutes to fight my way through all of the Warlord's minions. I hacked left and right with my sword and a minion dropped with every swing."

"That's the sword the king gave you the first time you saved the princess?" I asked.

"Of course! It was my most treasured possession, my boon companion, ever sharp and ever ready! It was in my hand for every fight and at my side for every kiss!"

"Yuck!" Billy said. He was only five and hadn't learned that kissing girls was something a hero sometimes had to suffer through if he was going to have adventures.

"My boy, there might come a day when you won't mind smooching a pretty girl or two!" Old Mr. Hart rocked back in his chair, laughing. He looked off over our heads, something he always did when he was trying to remember something. "Now, where was I?"

"Hacking and slashing your way through minions to get to the Warlord!" I said.

"Right you are, David." Mr. Hart rocked forward and then leaned even closer. "I fought on, but it seemed like the Warlord had a never ending supply of minions! For every one I cut down, two more popped up in his place. But I gained a step with every minion I killed until, at last, I finally broke free of all those underlings. Leaving them for the king's men to handle, I looked for the Warlord. Good ol' Roy was just a few seconds behind me and his sword was stained just as red as mine was.

*'Where is the Warlord, my Captain?'*

*'Looks like he's scarpered off, Roy.'*

"What's 'scarpered' mean?" Billy asked.

I hoped Billy learned all this important stuff soon. The rest of us were getting tired of him interrupting the story with stupid questions. But Mr. Hart never missed a beat.

"Good ol' Roy gave me a puzzled look.

*'Is that another of your colorful Terran words, my Captain?'*

"I laughed as we ran down a corridor we had just discovered, hidden behind the Warlord's throne.

*'Indeed it is, old friend! It means the Warlord has run away.'*

"Good ol' Roy boomed his famous laugh.

*'And so you have enriched our language yet again! Truly, is there nothing you cannot do, my Captain?'*

"Then we ran out the back door of the Warlord's palace and spied the evil overlord not thirty meters ahead of us!"

"Did he have Princess Audrey with him?" I asked. "Was she fighting him?"

"You got it, David! The Warlord had one huge hand wrapped around her slender wrist and was dragging her toward a boat waiting on the river. She was fighting him like a heckcat!"

"You said 'hellcat' last time," I reminded Mr. Hart.

"Last time your mother wasn't outside tending to her garden and close enough to hear everything I said," Mr. Hart said in a low voice. "Language like that is best kept for when it's only us men, don't you think?"

We all nodded. You couldn't expect girls, even if they were also moms, to understand guy talk!

"So, the beautiful Princess Audrey fought against the Warlord with every fiber of her lovely being, but the evil man was too strong for her! He dragged her closer and closer to the boat. More of his minions were on the boat, preparing to cast off. I knew if he got onto that boat, he would vanish into the jungle and the princess would be lost to me forever!"

"What did you do?" three of us asked in unison.

Mr. Hart smiled and leaned even closer. "What do you boys think I did?"

"I know!" Billy said. "You shot him with your Onesie!"

The rest of us rolled our eyes. Billy really needed to start paying attention to important details.

"I already used up the gun's single charge shooting the Shaman," Mr. Hart reminded him.

"Oh, yeah."

"Anybody else got a guess?"

All us older kids knew the answer, but it was Art's turn to say it. "You Boosted!"

Mr. Hart beamed at Art. "That's right, lad. I Boosted! I got a jolt as adrenaline poured into my blood stream. The pain from all the scrapes and stabs I'd gotten fighting the Warlord's minions disappeared and my fatigue was washed away!"

"What's that mean?" Billy whispered to Art.

"It means he didn't hurt any more and he wasn't tired," Art whispered back.

"With renewed strength, I bounded toward the Warlord."

*'Unhand the princess and fight me, Warlord!'*

"At the sound of my voice, Audrey's eyes met mine."

*'I knew you would come for me, my love!'*

"Her spirit was unbowed and, knowing I had come for her, Audrey struggled even harder to break free of the Warlord's iron grip.

"The Warlord realized he couldn't get to the boat before I caught up to him. With a sneer, he shoved the princess away from him and drew the huge sword he wore over his shoulder! The song of steel sliding free from its scabbard was music to my ears. At long last, after countless adventures, the Warlord and I were going to go toe-to-toe, blade–to–blade, man–to–man. It was our destiny and we knew only one of us could survive the battle!"

The five of us who were sitting on Mr. Hart's front porch gasped and scooted closer. We'd been listening to Mr. Hart's adventures all summer and *this* was the moment we'd all been waiting for!

"The Warlord was swinging his mighty sword even before I reached him. He knew his stuff, I'll give him that. The Warlord had timed the attack perfectly. I was charging right into the path of the blade! I heard Audrey cry out in fear as I brought my sword up to block the powerful blow. Steel met steel with a resounding clang. A lesser blade might have broken, leaving the man wielding it to be cut in two. A man whose heart was not fueled by the love of a beautiful woman might have crumpled under the awesome force of that blow. But my blade was great and my love was greater! The Warlord's blade was blocked.

"I rolled away, slashing at the Warlord's chest as I came back to my feet. My sword bit flesh–"

We all cheered.

"But the Warlord wasn't just strong, he was quick. He jumped back at the last second and my blade did nothing more than scratch his chest."

"Aw, no!" we moaned.

"But I was the first man to ever draw blood against the Warlord! He stared at the scratch as if I had cut his belly wide open. When he looked back at me, I saw fear in his eyes!

*'No man cuts me!'*

*'There's a first time for everything, Warlord. And I aim to cut you again and again until you've been whittled down to nothing!'*

*'Perhaps I have underestimated you, Hart. It is a mistake I will not make again.'*

*'There won't be a second time!'*

"Through all the talk, our blades had clashed again and again.

"Then the Warlord did the unexpected, the unthinkable! When we spun apart after a flurry of blows, he drew his dagger and hurled it right at the unprotected heart of Princess Audrey!"

"No! He can't kill the princess!" I cried. "Not after all you went through to save her!"

"He was the Warlord, David. What he could not possess, he destroyed! He knew the princess was mine, heart and soul, just as I was hers. He might have her, but he could never have her love. And at that moment and in that fight, he knew he could not defeat me. So he threw the dagger, hard and true, to kill the woman who meant everything to me!"

"Did– Did he kill her?" I asked in a voice barely above a whisper.

"I was afraid he had. I heard the knife bite flesh. I heard Audrey cry out. Fearing the worst, I turned toward her. The sight that met my eyes was seared into my brain, never to be forgotten. I can see it now as clearly as I did on that day so many years ago! A body lay crumpled on the ground, the dagger protruding from the body's chest. Blood welling up around the blade, turning everything around it crimson."

A far away look came into Mr. Hart's eye, as if he really was seeing it all over again.

"Oh no!" I breathed.

*'Do something, my love!'*

"Tears streaming from her eyes, Princess Audrey cradled the limp form of good ol' Roy in her arms.

*'He leapt in front of me and took the blade meant for me! Hurry, my love, you must save him!'*

"I looked around to see where the Warlord had gotten to. He was jumping into the boat as his men cast off.

*'We will meet again, Hart! And when we do, you will die!'*

"The Warlord got away?" Art asked.

"I'm afraid so," Mr. Hart said.

"But what happened to good ol' Roy?" I asked. "Did he die?"

"That's a story for another day, boys," Mr. Hart said, leaning back and starting to rock in his chair.

We protested, but once Mr. Hart went back to rocking there was no changing his mind. Story time was over for now. The other boys and I got up quietly. Mr. Hart's head was already drooping and the first snore came shortly after.

"That was the best adventure yet!" Art declared as we walked away.

There was no doubting that Art was right. Just as there was no doubting what I planned to do when I grew up. I was going to have adventures. I was going to fight evil warlords. I might even kiss a girl.

I was going to be a Scout!

SCOUT'S OATH

*Callan is Almost Four*

My room was messy. I knew Mommy wasn't going to like that. I would tell her that the mess wasn't my fault, but I'd tried that before. She never believed me before, but maybe she'd believe my new guard, Rob.

He could tell her about the bad men who came into my room. Maybe it would help that three of them were in here, lying on the floor. Two of them were really quiet. The third one was making a bubbly sound when he breathed. I wished he would stop because it sounded really creepy.

I cried when the men kicked open my door. It scared me *and* they'd knocked my dollhouse over. I spent all day getting the house just right and the bad men had ruined it.

Rob put me in my safe corner. Then he drew his sword and started fighting the men. My guard made me proud because he was a very good swordsman. Of course, Daddy only let good swordsmen guard me, so that wasn't a surprise. The worst thing was the fight was so loud it scared me even more. I covered my ears and cried louder.

It took a minute before I realized Rob was talking to me. I took my hands from my ears to listen. He was telling my favorite bedtime story, the one about the princess who fell in love with a hero from nowhere. Rob told the story better than any of my other guards, even though he was my newest guard. Rob did voices for everyone in the story and that made it sound a lot better. Listening to the story over the sound of the fight, I should have still been scared. But I had Rob fighting for me *and* telling my favorite story, so I wasn't scared at all. Or not as much, anyway.

When the third man fell down and started the bubbly breathing, the last two men ran away. Rob sat down in my safety nook and pulled me onto his lap.

"Are you all right, my princess?"

"Finish the story."

Rob smiled as if I had answered his question. And, as I wondered what Mommy would say about the mess, he finished the story.

Then Mommy and Daddy came running into my room. Mommy didn't say anything about the mess, she just ran to me and hugged me tight. I knew she was going to notice the mess sometime, so I brought it up.

"It's not my fault my room is messy, Mommy."

"What?" Mommy held me out so she could look at me and I saw she was crying.

"The mess isn't my fault. And it's not Rob's fault, either. Not really. Those men on the floor started the fight. Rob just fought back. And that's what he's supposed to, right? And he told me my favorite story. So the mess isn't my fault or Rob's fault."

Mommy's face got that funny look you get when you want to laugh and cry at the same time.

"Oh, Callie, I'm not worried about the mess. I'm worried about you!"

"Why? I had Rob with me and he kicked ass!"

The funny look on Mommy's face got funnier.

"Where did you hear that, young lady?"

"It's what the guards say when someone does a good job, Mommy."

"I see. I believe I shall have to have a word with your guards. Several words, in fact."

Rob cleared his throat. "If you'll permit me, Your Majesty, I shall convey your displeasure to the rest of Her Highness's guards. I will make your will crystal clear and in no uncertain terms, even if I have to kick them in the..."

Rob had forgotten the word, so I helped.

"Ass."

"Thank you, Your Highness, but I was going to say 'seat of the pants,' instead."

"Oh. Is that what I should be saying, Mommy?"

"It would be a good start, Callie."

I gave a big yawn.

"And we should get you to bed. How would you like to sleep with your father and me tonight?"

I laid my head on Mommy's shoulder. "Will Rob be there, too?"

"Tonight, I will be right outside your parents' door. But if you need me, I'll be there for you, Little One. I'll always be there for you."

I decided then and there that I was going to marry Rob. Or maybe the hero from nowhere. But I knew I was going to marry a hero.

# Chapter 1

*David*

Life settled down after Windslow's death. Raoul vanished, abandoning the crew of the *Kestrel* to the less than tender mercies of the Mordanian judicial system. Martin spent hours in the dungeon visiting with the crew. I don't know what he said to them, but I got the distinct idea the crew preferred Mordanian justice to whatever Martin had in mind.

Meanwhile, during the day I learned about the myriad duties expected of the consort to Her Highness, Princess Callan. Apparently, there's more to the job of prince consort than rescuing the princess and foiling kidnappings. Who knew?

At night, well, let's just say I learned other important things. It was a happy, busy, Boost-free life.

Four months after Callan's twenty-first birthday, harsh reality intruded on us again. Finding ourselves with a rare morning free of appointments, Callan and I had decided to enjoy some private time together. We'd given the servants the morning off and enjoyed a languorous few hours entwined in each other's arms. We had only recently arisen when a knock came at the door. Callan threw on a robe and padded to the door.

A page bowed when she opened the door. "I beg pardon, Your Highness. His Majesty summons you and Captain Rice to his council chambers."

"Thank you, Michael," she said. "Please tell my father we'll join him shortly."

As Callan shut the door, she said, "I wonder what this is all about?"

"Perhaps your father simply forgot we were going to stay in this morning," I suggested.

"Don't I wish! No, he and mother were all smiles when I told them our plans." Callan rolled her eyes. "Daddy, bless his heart, made some offhand remarks about an heir and pining for the patter of little feet."

I chuckled at the thought of how that conversation had gone.

Callan glared at me. "You only laugh because you weren't there when my mother added her advice."

"Oh? What did she suggest?"

"Mother was not subtle in the least." Callan shuddered, but then followed that with a wicked smile. "Based on your reaction this morning, though, her advice was spot on!"

My mouth dropped open. "Dare I ask *which* reaction you're grinning about?"

Callan leaned in close and whispered in my ear, "No."

My plan to pursue this line of inquiry further was interrupted by the arrival of our servants. Other pages must have been sent to alert them at the same time Michael was sent to us. To my surprise, the servants dressed us in formal court clothing rather than our less elaborate daily clothing. Callan's ladies-in-waiting spent an hour fussing with her hair and make-up before declaring her fit for court. Even then, they only stopped when Michael returned to find out what was taking us so long.

"What is this about, Daddy?" Callan asked when we joined her parents in the council chambers adjoining the court.

"An envoy from the city-state of Beloren has arrived and requested an audience," the king replied. "He specifically requested the two of you be present, as well."

I didn't care for the sound of that, nor did Callan. She took my hand in both of hers.

"What does he want?" she asked.

"I have no idea," her father replied, "but the navy reports he was escorted across the desert by a fleet numbering at least two hundred airships. All twenty-seven of the southern city-states are represented in the fleet. They stopped ten miles south of our border, allowing the envoy's ship to sail on by itself. Those ships are still there, holding position and, we assume, waiting for the envoy to return. The admiralty is understandably concerned about this. They are mobilizing every serviceable airship they can find."

Further conversation was cut off when a court functionary knocked and entered. "The envoy from Beloren awaits, Your Majesty."

We were announced to the formal court session and the chamberlain presented the envoy.

"Thank you for acceding to my request with such alacrity, Your Majesty." The envoy bowed deeply. "I shall come directly to the point of my visit. I have been sent seeking justice for the people of Beloren, justice for crimes most foul! The lords of the city request the extradition of the heinous criminal David Rice!"

# Chapter 2

*Callan*

My heart raced and my chest constricted as the envoy's words registered. I gripped David's hand tighter. He squeezed my hand once, letting his calm strength flow into me. As always, it worked. My heartbeat slowed and I found I could breathe normally again.

"I have no reason to believe your accusation is valid, envoy, especially when one takes into consideration *why* David Rice was in Beloren!" my father said.

Daddy always chose to be diplomatic, if possible. If I had been sitting on the throne—a seat I was in no hurry to assume—I'd have told the envoy where he could stuff his accusations and then have had him thrown out of the palace on his ear. A quick glance at Mom's face showed she felt the same way I did. Daddy probably did, too, but he was speaking for the kingdom rather than himself. That is just one reason it's not so easy being the monarch.

The envoy turned and looked David in the eyes. Then he turned and looked me *not* in the eyes. I've only met one man whose eyes met mine the first time we met. I married that man.

The envoy turned back to Daddy. "While I understand your reluctance to accept the truth, the facts are plain for all to see. They leave no doubt as to the guilt of your son–in–law!"

"We have a busy schedule today, Envoy," Daddy said. We didn't, which the envoy probably knew, but niceties must be observed. Daddy continued, "If you have facts of which we are not aware, then present them to us now."

"Of course, Your Majesty. Since that fateful day several months ago, numerous witnesses have come forward with stories of the attacks David Rice initiated against Beloren citizens," the envoy said.

My patience broke. "Come now, Envoy, why call them 'stories' when a far more precise word—'lies'—is available?"

Daddy frowned at me but Mom gave me an approving nod.

"Further more," the envoy raised his voice, "David Rice loosed a dangerous beast—a full-grown tammar—within the city walls. More than a dozen citizens were slain by the tammar. The resulting panic led to the ignition of a devastating fire. Many more citizens died in the fire, which eventually destroyed half of the city!"

"Only half?" I said. "That is rather disappointing news. David, shall we go back and finish the job?"

The envoy's voice rose a second time but his tone remained mild. I began to wonder if this speech was nothing more than a performance. "I am appalled at your callousness, Your Highness! You jest over death and destruction on a massive scale. King Edwar, have you spent no time training your heir in the art of diplomacy?"

Daddy had been keeping his temper in check, but that was the last straw. His face a mask of cold fury, Daddy rose to his feet and glared down at the envoy. "Those tunnel rats you call Beloren citizens are nothing more than a nest of criminals your government is too weak-willed to clean out! They planned to feed my daughter to that tammar for their own macabre entertainment, a point I notice you conveniently ignore. David did what your own city guards refuse to do—he entered that rat's nest to save an innocent life! Without David's 'unprovoked attack,' my daughter would be dead and, in the wake of my wrath, there would be nothing left of Beloren other than a few scribbled lines in dusty, unread history books!

"Now, Envoy, I strongly suggest you scurry back to your pathetic little city-state before I *really* lose my temper," Daddy thundered. "Should you have the misfortune to witness such an occurrence, you will think my daughter a model of tact and decorum in comparison!"

"There is one last detail I must mention, Your Majesty," the envoy smiled thinly. "If I do not return with Captain Rice in my custody, that fleet off your southern border will immediately attack Mordan!"

# Chapter 3

*David*

"Do not make absurd and meaningless threats, man!" King Edwar said. "Our navy is much larger, much stronger, and our crews much better trained than anything your motley collection of city–states could hope to send against us. Your fleet cannot possibly win a war with Mordan!"

"Everything you say is true, Your Majesty. And yet the fleet *will* attack if I do not return with Captain Rice in custody!" the envoy said.

"But why would you throw away lives and airships without even the hope of victory?" King Edwar betrayed his bafflement at the envoy's intransigence. The same look was reflected on the courtiers present and, I'm sure, my own face.

The envoy cast a furtive glance around the court then lowered his voice. "Perhaps I could shed some light on this matter if we spoke privately."

"I have no secrets from those present in these chambers. You may speak freely before them."

The envoy's voice remained low. "If word of what I wish to tell you reaches the wrong ears, my family will be endangered."

"You show precious little concern for *my* family. Why should I be concerned for yours?"

"Please!" The envoy bowed in supplication.

My father–in–law glared at the envoy for a good fifteen seconds. The man held his bow the whole time.

"Clear the chamber," the king said to his chamberlain. A moment later, we were alone with the envoy.

"I have acceded to your request, Envoy," King Edwar said. "Now explain what is behind this insane threat of yours!"

"The lords of the twenty–seven city–states have no desire to wage war against Mordan. Unfortunately, they fear the aftermath of a war with Mordan far less than they fear a threat within their own city walls," the envoy told us. "What do you know of those we call the tunnel rats?"

Callan spoke, "They are a murderous rabble your lords are too uncaring or too weak-willed to eradicate!"

"I understand why you hold that opinion, Your Highness, but it is far removed from the truth of the matter," the envoy said.

"Then explain it so we may understand," the king said.

"The tunnel rats have been a problem among the various city states for generations. Any city with long-abandoned sewers and catacombs has some criminal element who find safety and shelter in such places. Even Morda, your own capital city, is said to have criminal lairs hidden beneath its streets! But the city-states stood for centuries before men settled this far north. The network of tunnels beneath Beloren dwarfs Morda's catacombs. The same holds true for the other city-states.

"For centuries, the lords of the city-states attempted to drive out or destroy the tunnel rats hiding beneath our streets. Traditional military units fare poorly underground. Their training and tactics are ill-suited to such missions. Invariably, they fail to eradicate the tunnel dwellers, losing too many men in the process," the envoy said.

"If it was just a matter of training," I said, "why not devise proper training and create an elite unit to combat the tunnel rats?"

"Because the tunnel rats, while irritating, did not cause sufficient trouble to be worth the extra expense of such training," the envoy replied. "In retrospect, it was short-sighted of them."

"Really? What was your first clue?" Callan's tone was thick with sarcasm.

"Are you implying what my daughter went through isn't considered 'enough trouble' to be worth the attention of the lords of Beloren?" King Edwar's tone matched that of his daughter.

"No, Your Majesty, I most assuredly am not implying that. That rationalization ended twenty years ago. The lords of Beloren, wishing to be viewed as 'doing something' about the tunnel rat problem, hired a mercenary named Vraal to take care of the criminal infestation in the tunnels.

"Vraal led his band of violent, ruthless men into the abandoned sewers and killed the leaders of the tunnel rats. I must assume Vraal liked what he found in the tunnels. Instead of claiming the balance of his fee from the lords, he declared himself King Rat and took control of the city–state's criminal element," the envoy said. "Over the next ten years, he has found ways to extend his control beyond Beloren's walls and into the tunnels under the other twenty–six city–states. For the last ten years, he has wielded enormous power throughout all of the southern city–states. It is true the lords administer the city–states, but they do so at the forbearance of King Rat.

"Over the years, King Rat has expanded the tunnels, building new underground passages throughout each of the city–states. His messengers can pass unseen into the most secure rooms in Beloren. His assassins do so, as well," the envoy said. "Vraal wants Captain Rice and doesn't care how much blood must be spilled to get him. The lords would rather have thousands of their subjects slain in a war with Mordan than have their families slain in their beds!"

Thousands dead? How many of them would be Mordanian? I could not allow death on such a scale when it was within my power to stop it!

I stepped forward. "You may call off your fleet, Envoy. I will surrender myself to you!"

# Chapter 4

*Callan*

As David's announcement echoed in the vast court chamber, the envoy from Beloren and my parents stood there and blinked in astonishment. I'd had a feeling he was going to say something noble and selfless. That meant I was the first to react to his words. My reaction was going to be emotional, but I was unwilling to start crying before the odious envoy. So I chose to react with anger and punched David in the arm.

"Ouch!" he said, rubbing his arm.

"Before you make such a bold pronouncement in the future," I said, "I strongly suggest you discuss it with your wife, first!"

"There wasn't anything to discuss, Callan, because I had only one honorable choice!" David said.

He can be *so* annoying when he decides to be noble!

"How can you stand there and tell me—your wife—that there was nothing to discuss?"

"The day after we met, I swore an oath to you and to Rob, pledging to protect your life with mine," David said. "When we were married, my oath to you extended to your family and your kingdom. If I stand firm against the envoy's ludicrous claims—"

The envoy found his tongue. "Ludicrous? Now just—"

"Shut. Up." I snarled at the envoy. "Ludicrous is far too polite a word to describe the charges you have presented to us. I was raised to behave as a proper princess should behave, otherwise I'd have used a long string of single-syllable words instead. I was surrounded by guardsmen from the moment I was born. I learned quite a collection of improper words from them, all of which are far more appropriate to this situation than my husband's innocuous choice of words!"

I only realized I had stalked into the envoy's face when David caught my arm and gently pulled me into his embrace.

Then David looked me in the eyes and said, "My love, thousands of men will die if we go to war with the city–states. Parents will lose sons. Wives will lose husbands. Children will lose fathers.

"In a war to defend the entire country against another nation's attacks, such losses are necessary. In a war to defend a single man, such losses are," and here he gave me his infuriating, irresistible smile, "a string of single–syllable words inappropriate for a proper princess to use."

What could I say to that? Dozens of men had died attempting to defend me from the kidnapping plot of the former Tartegian queen. I would always bear the burden of their deaths. How could I wish a far heavier burden on David? I leaned my head against his chest, let go of my anger, and let my tears flow.

"David," my father said, "you do not need to do this. To a man, our military will defend you and Mordan against this rabble from the city–states. To a man, they will *want* to defend you, son!"

"I know they will, Your Majesty," David said, "but I cannot allow sacrifices on such a massive scale for a single man. Even if I were willing to allow the men to fight and die for me, it makes no sense from a military or political point of view. While I have no doubt our navy would rout the city–states' fleet with comparative ease, it would distract and weaken us at a time when tensions remain high with Tarteg."

Daddy gazed at David for a moment and then nodded his head. "Very well. I will defer to your wishes in this matter."

Still holding me in his embrace, David spoke to the envoy. "We will depart tomorrow morning, Envoy. I would spend a last night with my wife."

Then David took my hand and led me back to our chambers for our final hours together.

# Chapter 5

*David*


Even in a royal palace, you'd think it would be possible for a man to retreat to his chambers to spend a few hours alone with his wife. This should be especially true when the man is going away for who knows how long the next morning! I was fortunate enough to have an entire palace full of people eager to show me just how wrong I was.

The first knock came no more than a minute after we'd shut the door. I had just pulled Callan into an embrace and was leaning in to kiss her when knuckles rapped on the door. Unable to ignore her royal training, Callan tried to pull away to answer the knock. I tightened my embrace, pulling her even closer.

"Ignore the door, dear," I breathed into her ear. "After a few minutes, whoever is out there will figure out that we don't want to be disturbed and go away!"

Our prospective visitors not only didn't go away, they called through the door.

"Callie? David? Please let us in!"

It was Callan's parents. I know they wanted to comfort their only child and her husband, but I also knew they wanted a grandchild and heir to the throne. You'd think they would give us a chance—perhaps our last chance—to try to provide one for them. Callan looked toward the door and when she pulled away this time, I released her.

Callan's mother swept her daughter into a hug, speaking soft words of comfort to her. My father-in-law surprised me by wrapping me in a fierce hug, as well.

"Like most fathers, I was certain no man would ever be good enough to marry my daughter—not even Prince Rupor!" Edwar said as he released me. "You proved me wrong when you rescued Callan. You proved me wrong again when you rescued Elaina and me. And now you've proven me wrong a third time. Do me a favor, lad. When

112

you get back from Beloren—and I'm certain you *will* get back—stop trying so hard to show me the error of my ways!"

"If you can get the rest of the planet to cooperate, I'll be more than happy to do as you ask," I replied, flashing my first genuine smile since we received the king's summons to court.

"I shall bend every ruler and diplomat to my will in an attempt to do as you ask, David." The king gave me a knowing smile. "Callie and Elaina will expect no less from me."

Once again, the king and queen offered to wage war against the city–states. Then they traded back and forth, offering words of comfort and concern. What they did not do was offer to leave us alone. By the time the king and queen finally ran out of words and hugs and took their leave of us, word of my decision had spread throughout the capital. Our friends dropped everything to visit and offer their deepest consolation in this difficult time.

What I found most difficult about the time was finding some way to spend it with Callan. But I was polite and kept that thought to myself.

Don't get me wrong, I love my friends and family dearly. I very much wanted to say goodbye to Tristan and Nist. I wanted to tousle Milo's hair and to make sure he and Kim knew that, with or without me, they would always have a place in the palace. I wanted to ask Martin what he knew about Beloren's tunnel rats. But I planned to arise early the next morning and do all that before leaving with the envoy. Other than those few people, I could have happily gone without seeing anyone else from the palace.

I grew heartily tired of hearing visitor after visitor tell me how selfless and heroic I was. My arm grew tired shaking all of the proffered hands. My facial muscles felt as if they had frozen into the perpetual smile I wore for Callan's sake. It took all of my self control not to shout at everyone to go away and leave us alone. And it took hours to clear our chambers of all of our unwanted well–wishers. Only then did I have Callan all to myself.

I locked the door to our chambers and then kissed Callan deeply. As always when I held her in my arms, time went away and Callan and I were as one.

The next morning, Callan and I walked hand in hand to the palace docks. With an honor guard before us and most of the palace population behind us, I kissed Callan one last time. I tilted Callan's head back and gazed deeply into her eyes.

"I *will* be back, my love."

"You had better be," she whispered fiercely.

As I turned away from my wife, light flashed from polished steel as the blades of the honor guard snapped up into a sharp, silver arch. Passing beneath the crossed swords, I looked straight ahead. A moment later, I boarded the Beloren airship and left behind all I had ever known and loved in this world.

# Chapter 6

*Callan*

I promised myself I would not let David see me cry. I kept that promise until the honor guard formed up along David's path. When their swords flashed, forming the arch beneath which he walked, tears welled up in my eyes. My vision blurred and I found it impossible to see clearly. I blinked the tears away, only to have them return immediately. I refused to wipe them away, just in case David looked back. His last sight of me must not be that of a girl, weeping for her lost love. It must be that of a woman, determined to be reunited with her husband.

Perhaps David suspected what he would see in my eyes if he looked back at me. Perhaps he struggled to control tears of his own. Perhaps he refused to give the Beloren envoy the satisfaction of an emotional reaction. Whatever the reason, David strode forward, head held high and faced forward.

Only when he stood on the deck of the Beloren airship did David cast a final look at me. By then, he was too far away to see my tears, which flowed like rivers down my cheeks. Two Beloren airmen took him below deck while the rest of the crew cast off. The airship's engines roared to life. Through my tears, I stood and watched the airship rise from the courtyard. Through my tears, I watched as the airship turned to face south. Through my tears, I watched the airship steam over the palace rooftops and pass from sight.

Turning back to the palace, I wasn't surprised to find my parents standing a few paces behind me. Without a word, they gathered me into their arms. I released my grief and sobbed as I had not done since I was a little girl.

Some moments later, I kissed my parents on their cheeks and offered them a brave smile. With my eyes dry, I walked back to the chambers David and I shared. Everyone I met along the way bowed or saluted, each of them showing respect for my grief and respect for

David's sacrifice. I offered a smile and a nod to each of them and felt immense relief when I reached our chambers.

Entering my room, I found Martin leaning casually against the balcony door, his arms folded. Tristan, Nist, and Milo were arrayed along the wall beside him.

"He's gone," I whispered.

Martin said, not unkindly, "Your Highness, you didn't ask us to meet you here just to tell us what we could see with our own eyes."

"No, Martin, I didn't," I said. "I asked you here because I need a fast airship and the most daring of pilots. I need a doctor who knows the desert. I need a young thief who knows life on a city's streets. And I need a reformed raider who knows Beloren's darkest secrets."

I looked them each in the eye, "I am going to Beloren to get my husband back, but I cannot do that without your help. Are you with me?"

"You don't even need to ask, lass," Tristan said.

"But just in case there's any doubt, I'll give you our answer," Martin added. "Damned right we're with you!"

# Chapter 7

*Callan*

The problem with secret rescue plans is you have to spend time making the plans. I didn't want to spend hours discussing how best to slip into Beloren unnoticed or how to get one of us down among the tunnel rats. I wanted to board the *Pauline* and fly off after David *right now*.

I could see it all in my mind's eye. We would catch up with the Envoy's airship. Nist would bring the *Pauline* alongside the airship. Then Martin would Boost, we'd all storm aboard, and...probably all die grisly deaths.

I have never been good at this kind of planning. I prefer to skip all that tedious thinking ahead stuff and get straight to the action. That's why my father has always surrounded me with thoughtful guards and advisors. In the past, Rob kept me focused and forced me to plan my actions. David had done it since Rob's death and, I hoped, would do it for me again when we came home. Today, I counted on Martin and Tristan. They were thorough—painstakingly, mind numbingly thorough.

"Milo," I asked, when I was no longer able to concentrate on their endless discussion, "when will Kim be here?"

"She said she would come right up after completing her etiquette lesson with Lady Andrea," he said.

"Very good. And you told her what I'm asking you to do?" I asked. "She must give her permission for you to come along.

"Yes, Your Highness, I have her permission to go," he said, rolling his eyes. "She knows you'll do everything in your power to keep me safe, blah blah blah." He grinned, "Kim did show real concern when I told her about the rescue—but only when I told her Nist was going to be your pilot."

Nist's eyes went wide. "Your sister is worried about *me*?"

"I told you he'd never figure it out, Milo," Tristan sighed. "Nist has spent too much time flying me around on that airship and too little time courting the fairer sex. The lad claims he can see the wind but he can't see the love written on a pretty girl's face!"

Nist's face went crimson at his adopted father's words, but Tristan was right. Nist was the only person in the palace who hadn't a clue about Kim's feelings.

A complicated knock came from the door—the signal Milo had given Kim. Milo opened the door and his sister slipped into the room. One glance at Nist told Kim everything.

Blushing to match Nist, Kim whirled on her little brother, "You told him!"

"Of course I told him. I'd have been an old man in my twenties if I waited for Nist to figure it out or for you to make the first move!" Milo said.

Martin gently shoved Nist toward Kim. "Why don't you take the blushing beauty out on the balcony. Perhaps the two of you could *talk* to each other for while?"

Milo flashed a mischievous grin. "Nist, as Kim's only male relative, I grant you permission to kiss my sister if you want."

Both of them blushed even deeper, but they went out onto the balcony. Nist even took Kim's hand just before pulling the balcony door shut behind them.

Martin turned serious. "Tristan and I have worked out a plan, Callan."

"Tell me," I said.

"Remember when we robbed the treasury to pay for my airships?" Martin asked. When I nodded, he continued, "We need to rob the treasury again. No, it's more like *I* need to rob it. And I need to 'steal' more than a fistful of cut gems."

"Spill it, Martin!" I said. "What do you have in mind?"

Martin drew in a breath, as if preparing to deliver bad news. "I need to steal the Mordanian crown jewels!"

# Chapter 8

*Callan*

Steal my country's crown jewels? Was Martin insane? I opened my mouth to ask that very question—and then shut my mouth again. Martin was many things, but I had no doubts about his sanity. Besides, Tristan had helped concoct this plan. The good doctor is a romantic, but, as my father frequently says, he is also quite a sober, sane, and sensible man. If Martin and Tristan thought we needed the crown jewels, I would hear them out before offering an opinion.

Before I could ask Martin to explain further, a knock sounded on the door to my chambers. Who could it be? Everyone in the palace must know I had shut myself in my room to mourn for David!

"Callie?" It was my mother. Of course. Who else would come knocking at a time like this? "May I come in, dear?"

After I had waited so long for Martin and Tristan to conceive of a rescue plan for David, Mom had to show up and delay their explanation further. My mother certainly had great timing! I shooed Martin, Tristan, and Milo out to the balcony while also calling out in an emotion–laden voice, "Just a minute, Mother!"

I only called her 'Mother' when I was upset. I felt a tinge of pride at that added touch. Then I remembered I truly *was* upset. It hadn't even crossed my mind to call her 'Mom.'

"Keep quiet out there," I hissed to my conspirators, closing the balcony doors.

On my way to let Mother in, I mussed my hair and worked up a few tears. Planning the rescue had pushed the grief into the back of my mind, but it came rushing back as soon as I tried to look grief–stricken. Hanging my head, I opened the door.

"Y–yes, Mother?"

Mom shook her head, tutting. "Look at you, shut up in here and crying your eyes out! You poor dear."

Mom raised her eyebrows, wordlessly asking why she was still standing in the hallway.

"Come in, Mother."

Mom breezed in and made a beeline for the balcony! "It's so dreary in here, Callie! A little light and a little fresh air will make you feel better."

"I don't want light. I don't want fresh air. And I don't want to feel better!" I sounded like a petulant child, even to myself.

"Pish and tosh, dear," Mother said, reaching for the door handles.

In a rush, I slipped between Mom and the doors and threw my arms around her. Burying my face in her shoulder, I tried for the same wracking sobs I'd had in the courtyard. My mother spun me around as effortlessly as she had when I was five. She ended up facing me and with her back to the balcony doors. Reaching behind herself, she turned the knobs and threw the doors open.

"Martin," Mother said, still watching me, "why don't you and the others come inside? After that, I'd like my daughter to tell me what is going on."

Releasing my mother, I looked her in the eye. "What do you think is going on, Mother? We're all going after David. Everyone except Kim. She's going to stay in these chambers and pretend to be me. With a little luck, she can keep it up long enough for us to rescue my husband."

Much as I hated it, the next thing I said came out in the wheedling tone of voice I used on her—to little effect—when I was a young child. "Please don't try to stop us!"

"Dearest daughter, I wouldn't dream of trying to stop you!"

Who was this woman and what had she done with my mother?

"You wouldn't?"

A slight smile played across Mom's face. "Whether I like it or not, you're not my little girl any more. You're a newlywed young woman, forcibly separated from your husband by cruel events beyond your control. You'd never forgive me if I did anything to interfere with your plans! And you would be quite right to do so."

"So, you're not going to place me under guard or lock me away in a tower or anything like that?"

"Goodness gracious, no, Callan! Where do you come up with these ideas?"

"So why are you here?"

"I came here to ask you a question."

"What question is that, Mother?"

"What can I do to help?"

# Chapter 9

*Callan*

"You want to help us?" I asked.

"Yes, Callie."

"With our plan to rescue David?"

"Well, I certainly didn't come up here to help you with your embroidery."

To my surprise, I laughed. I hated embroidery with every fiber of my being, something Mom knew all too well.

"Why are you so surprised, dear? David is a member of our family, now, and we *always* take care of family! Besides, your father and I are quite taken with the young man." The corners of Mom's mouth quirked up. "On top of that, you're quite smitten with him, as well. Those grandchildren your father and I want will arrive all the sooner if you're, shall we say, *enthusiastic* about spending time with your husband."

I felt a blush climb my cheeks. Who knew my mother had such a bawdy imagination? Well, I suppose my father knew. And I stopped *that* line of thought before it could go any farther. There are some things a child simply shouldn't know about her parents!

"Rescue before reunion, okay Mother?" I turned to my friends. "Martin, how can my mother help us?"

Martin didn't beat around the bush. "It would be much easier to get our hands on the crown jewels with your mother's help."

"Why, pray tell, do you need our crown jewels?"

Mom's tone of voice was curious rather than accusatory. Was it possible she would be willing to risk the crown jewels in the hopes of getting David back?

"There are a lot of people—many of them within this very palace—who have been waiting for me to revert to my raider form," Martin said, "I thought I would live down to their expectations in a

122

big way. I'll use my new found status as a friend of the royal family to move freely about the palace, take callous advantage of the distraction David's surrender has caused, and steal the crown jewels. Having completed this nefarious deed, it would surprise no one if I fled back to my old home port of Beloren. *Stealing* the jewels should get me back in the good graces of Beloren's criminal class. *Having* the jewels should allow me to gain an audience with King Rat."

"With an eye toward trading the crown jewels for David?" Mom said.

"Some of the crown jewels, yes. Most of them, even. But there must be some profit for me. After burning my Mordanian bridges so thoroughly, no one would believe me otherwise."

"You've fought tooth and nail to show all Mordan that you're a changed man. Would you really risk ruining your hard-won, barely-rehabilitated reputation just for the chance to rescue David?" Mom asked.

"Yes, Your Majesty, and without a second thought."

"I rather suspected that would be your answer. David is a truly remarkable young man and, if you ask me, quite deserving of such loyalty." She got that far away look which meant she was thinking. "Would you be willing to have a naval squadron chase you south? Just among ourselves, we will know it's an escort for Callan. As an added bonus, with you and the crown jewels inside Beloren's walls, the squadron will have an excellent excuse to stay nearby."

Martin nodded. "That's a *very* nice touch, Your Majesty!"

"Raiders aren't the only people who can be devious, Martin." Mom turned to me, "You said you were leaving Kim behind?"

"Yes, she's going to stay in these chambers and pretend to be me. The distraught princess who has shut herself away in the bedroom, just like in the fairy tales you used to read to me," I said. "With luck, no one will even know I'm gone until after we have David back."

Mom nodded, "I can help Kim with that. I'll be the doting queen trying to comfort the distraught princess, also just like in the fairy tales."

Mom turned to Martin and Tristan. "Gentlemen, let's discuss the details of this plan. I want to make sure we've done everything possible to insure my daughter's safety and my son-in-law's safe return!"

I groaned. Knowing how thorough my mother could be, I began to suspect it would be long past dark before we got under way.

Sometime in the afternoon, Mom sent for Daddy. He had more than a few suggestions for improving the plan. Most of those suggestions involved keeping me safely in the palace. The fifth time he made such a suggestion, I lost my temper.

"Daddy, that's enough! I'm going on this mission, whether you like it or not. And if you suggest I stay behind one more time, I swear I won't name my first born son after you!"

My father laughed. "That's not much of a threat, Callie. Everyone in the kingdom knows you're going to name your first born son after Rob."

He was right, blast him. So I just crossed my arms and turned the full force of my princess glare on him.

Daddy heaved a dramatic sigh. "Very well, Callie, I shall limit my suggestions to the course of action you've already chosen."

Finally, as the clock struck midnight, Nist piloted the *Pauline* to my balcony.

Climbing aboard the airship, I looked south. "Hang on, David. We're coming!"

# Chapter 10

*David*

As soon as I boarded the envoy's ship, two crewmen led me below deck and locked me into a small cabin. My cabin faced the palace, but the porthole was closed and locked. I wasn't even allowed one last look at Callan as we flew away. This pettiness was at odds with the near-pleading tone the envoy had taken when speaking privately with the royal family. It also proved indicative of my treatment while aboard the envoy's airship.

Crewmen intentionally dropped my food then kicked it across the deck with filthy bare feet. They'd spit into my water or drink it all while standing before me. It was the kind of casual cruelty displayed by the powerless when they are given dominion over some small aspect of another man's life. As a refined member of a royal family, the crewmen expected to horrify me with such behavior. They expected me to choose noble privation over accepting such tainted food and drink. I ate and drank everything I was given and relished the disappointment displayed by the crewmen at each meal. Had they seen what I had eaten during academy survival training, they'd have thrown up their hands in despair—right after throwing up their last meal.

Just as the sun was setting, the envoy's airship rejoined the vast, motley fleet from the southern city-states. The shouts between airships, the dull roar of boiler fires, and the wail of whistles blowing off steam were my first clues we were among the fleet. This cacophony served as my constant companion for three days as the fleet crossed a thousand miles of desert. The calls of the crewmen served another purpose, as well. My implant assimilated and translated the language of the city-states by the end of the first day of the trip.

The implant imprinted the language before the sun rose on our second day of travel. By the time we reached Beloren, I understood everything the crew said and could have conversed with them, had I chosen to do so. I kept that fact to myself, pretending ignorance as crewmen laced their commands with vile insults. Language fluency was one of the two advantages I had over the tunnel rats. Boost, which I hadn't used the first time I was in Beloren, was the other.

To pass the long, hot days, I catalogued everything I knew or could guess about King Rat. The list was short, depressingly so. Based on the Envoy's statements in his private audience with the royal family, King Rat exerted complete control over his people. There was no sympathy to be found among the tunnel rats. Even without King Rat's iron rule, I was an outsider entering an insular and paranoid society. Once in the tunnels, I would be on my own.

To what I had been told and what I had guessed, I added what I had seen in my brief time in the tunnels. King Rat went in for over-the-top execution spectacles. No doubt, the blood and terror served multiple purposes—entertainment for tunnel rats, reinforcement for the us-versus-everyone-else sense of isolation, and a warning to any subjects who chafed under King Rat's rule.

Gruesome as it was, the man's love of spectacle was my primary source of hope. I had no doubt King Rat planned a brutal death for me, but my execution would be a special occasion. It had to be. When I rescued Callan and Raoul from the rat king's tammar pit, I dealt a serious blow to his pride and weakened his grip on this people. King Rat would make an example of me, but that example would be the main event in a day filled with blood and slaughter. No doubt, he would begin with a warmup act of lesser executions. After all, a proper spectacle requires a lot of pleading, a lot of blood, and a lot of corpses. With filled prisoner cages and the tunnel rats boiling over with excitement, what else could the rat ruler do but bow to the will of his people and stage his carnival of carnage?

I had a few days to find a way to kill King Rat. And I concluded I had no choice but to kill him. Left alive and still in power, King Rat would simply intimidate the lords of the city-states again. In short order, we'd be right back where we currently were. Maybe there would be some tunnel rat tradition I could call on, some way of forcing him to fight me. Maybe I could find an ambitious underling whose yearning for power exceeded his hatred of outsiders. Maybe I could do a lot of things, but I wouldn't know what those things were until I was underground.

At last, we docked in Beloren. The crewmen bound my hands and, led by the envoy, took me to the slave market. Silent crowds lined the streets, watching their official deliver me to the tunnel rats. It was yet another spectacle. It was yet another demonstration of King Rat's power over the city. The envoy led me directly to the entrance to the tunnels and, without ceremony, ordered me lowered into the darkness.

# Chapter 11

*David*

Hands rose out of the darkness and caught me. They untied the rope binding me and dragged me along the tunnel. As my eyes adjusted to the darkness, I recognized the tunnels through which my captors led me. They were leading me toward the tammar's arena, to where I had almost lost Callan and where Rob, her personal bodyguard and the most courageous man I had ever known, gave his life to save hers.

Could my guesses about King Rat have been wrong? Was it possible he cared more about revenge than spectacle? Could he consider me so dangerous he would choose a quick execution over a blood–soaked lesson for his subjects?

Then my captors led me past the tunnel which went to the arena and down a different one. Perhaps my assessment of King Rat had been correct, after all. At the end of the new tunnel, two guards stood before a door. One guard threw open the door as we approached and the other stepped inside ahead of us.

"The prisoner has arrived," the guard announced.

In my first visit, the arena was bright with massed torchlight. The throne room, if that's what this was, was the opposite. Lanterns spread dim pools of light every twenty feet or so, hiding the size of the room and providing deep shadows to mask the identity of those who attended the court of King Rat. The crowd was large but quiet, nothing like the frenzied mob I'd seen in the arena many months before. On the far side of the room, surrounded by the only bright lanterns in the room, stood a large chair. On the throne, for that was obviously what it was intended to be, sat a man no more than a few years older than Martin.

The two of us regarded each other with interest. The man before me was lean and smoothly muscled. He looked wiry and quick. I had no doubt he'd be a wily and capable fighter. I'd expected a brute of a man, tall and broad and starting to go fat. King Rat was nothing like I expected. The feeling appeared to be mutual.

"You're not all that impressive, now that I see you close up. And you're shorter than I remember," he said, speaking in accented Mordanian. "Of course, you're standing still this time, so it's easier to get a good look at you."

"I didn't notice you at all, last time," I replied, also in Mordanian. "I was rather busy and, truth to tell, not interested in sight-seeing. Not that your little kingdom would be a tourist high point, anyway."

"Ha!" He slapped his knee. "And you're not scared of me!"

I affected a puzzled look. "I must admit that you've lost me. As a member of one of the most powerful royal families on Aashla, why should I be scared of you?"

"I sent for you and here you are." King Rat leaned back in his throne, a satisfied look on his face. "*That* is power, little princeling."

"It's prince consort, not prince and certainly not princeling."

"Do not banter semantics with me, boy. You have been given to me and are now mine to do with as I wish!"

"You are sorely deluded if you think I was given to you," I said. "You live and breathe because I convinced my father-in-law your ragtag fleet, this half-destroyed city, and this pathetic sewer kingdom of yours were not worth destroying. I came here of my own volition, *not* because a rat pretending to be a king sent for me!"

"Is that so?" sneered King Rat. "Pray tell, why are you here?"

"I have come to challenge you, before these witnesses, to a duel to the death for that ratty throne you're sitting on," I said.

"You are a well-spoken young man. I'll give you that," King Rat said. "You must have been working on that challenge for hours."

"Yes, I'm a traditionalist to the core. Mentioning that, I notice you haven't answered my challenge. Do you accept?"

"Of course not."

"What's the matter?" I asked. "Are you too afraid to face me, Vraal?"

"No, boy, I'm too smart to face you without need." Vraal turned to the men who'd brought me into the throne room. "Throw him in the cell with the other one."

Vraal's men dragged me from his presence. I'd had no expectation the man would accept my challenge. There had been the slim hope I could make him lose his temper, though. I hadn't managed that, but I had not come away from our discussion empty handed, either. A blind man could see the rat king thought highly of himself. He rightly believed he wielded power beyond his tunnels, but he was sadly mistaken just how far his power extended on the surface world. Well, when you rule in an echo chamber, it's easy to fall prey to your own propaganda.

The guards led me through dozens of twists and turns and then walked me up and down hundreds of stairs. Disorientation was the intention behind the twists and turns, the climbing and descending. Without my implant, the plan would have succeeded admirably. Instead, I had my implant start recording a map of the rat kingdom's tunnels. Nearly thirty minutes later, we stopped next to a heavy door. A guard fished keys from a pocket and unlocked the door. The lantern–bearing guard shined just enough light through the door for my captors to chain me to the wall. The door clanged shut and absolute darkness cloaked the room.

"Hello?" called a voice from the darkness. "Who's there?"

"Well, my sins really are coming back to haunt me!" I said. "What are you doing down here, Raoul!"

# Chapter 12

*David*

"Rice?" Raoul asked, his voice rising in the darkness. "Is it really you?"

"Of course not. King Rat held a David Rice sound–alike contest and I won," I said in a monotone. "The prize was a stay in this cell with you."

"Oh," Raoul replied, his voice dropping. His voice was so filled with dejection, I could imagine his head hanging and his shoulders drooping.

"For God's sake, you moron, of course it's me!" I snapped. "What's the matter with you?"

Raoul gave a shuddering sigh, "I've been down here for a long time and had given up hope that anyone would come to rescue me, much less someone such as you."

"Rescue you? Are you out of your mind?" I wouldn't cross the street to rescue Raoul. There was no way I'd cross a desert to do it! "Have you forgotten the time you tried to get an airship captain and his crew to kill me? Or how about when you abandoned Callan, my friends, and me to the tender mercies of the trogs? Or kidnapped Callan's parents and–"

"Forget I said anything, Rice," Raoul snarled. He did sound much more like his usual self, at least.

"I'd love to forget you, Raoul, but you keep horning in on my life!" I said. I took a deep breath, reining in my temper. "But that doesn't matter right now. I'm as much a guest here as you."

"So you got captured, too?" Raoul asked. "I'm sure Callan is worried sick for her missing lover."

"Husband, as you well know," I corrected.

"I had held out hope that King Edwar would regain his senses after taking the time to think through the prospect of a commoner for an in-law. I have no doubt my father and brother would have

131

given all due consideration to renewing Rupor and Callan's betrothal if approached diplomatically."

"What a brilliant idea, Raoul! After all, only *half* of the Tartegian royal house conspired to kidnap Mordan's princess and heir to the throne. After you add in an unknown number of your mother's accomplices concealed within the Tartegian court, you have quite a strong argument in favor of Callan marrying into your family. It's all so clear to me now! I cannot imagine why you were the only one to see it with such clarity!"

Raoul lapsed into silence. My ridicule had, no doubt, hurt his prickly little feelings. I most assuredly hoped that was the case. Raoul's steadfast refusal to recognize just how thoroughly he and his mother had screwed up Rupor's betrothal never ceased to amaze me. But Raoul was the least of my worries.

Freed at last from listening to Raoul's nonsensical blather, I turned my attention to more pressing concerns. I pondered my options for escape, fantasized about what I'd do to King Rat if given the chance, and waited for something to happen.

An hour after Raoul stopped talking to me, I found another reason to dislike the man. He snored. Raoul's deep-throated roar did not quite bring the walls down around us, but it made it nearly impossible for me to sleep.

According to my implant, twenty-two hours passed before a guard arrived to take me back to the throne room. As I was led away, Raoul begged the guards to leave him a light. The guards laughed at the exiled prince and mocked his desperation. In spite of myself, I felt a twinge of pity for Raoul. It was no more than a twinge, mind you, but it was the first time in months I felt anything beyond loathing for the Spare Prince.

The guards led me up and down stairs and through a new set of twists and turns. Smiling to myself, I added this new information to the map being built by my implant. Entering the throne room, the map and the last few twists and turns were driven from my mind. I could not believe what I saw.

Martin Bane stood before King Rat!

# Interlude

*Callan is Ten*

I leaned my back against a support beam in the loft of the barn. My arms stretched around behind the rough column of wood, my shoulders aching from the discomfort. I looked to the ladder on the far side of the loft. Where was my hero? Why had he not come? Why had he forsaken me in my hour of need?

This was intolerable! My nose itched and I had straw tangled in my hair. What kind of champion would leave his princess in such distress?

I sighed and pulled my arms from around the beam. The pain in my shoulders eased as my right hand scratched the tip of my nose. I ran a hand through my hair but found it so tangled my fingers caught and pulled at my hair. Well, ladies–in–waiting had to have something to do when I got back to my room, right?

I'd just have to make Mom understand I made a mess of myself out of deep concern that the ladies–in–waiting would be released from service if they had nothing to do. Maybe Daddy would be there instead of Mom. If he was, I could just whip up a few tears, he'd melt, and so would my problems. Of course, all was lost if Rob was on duty tonight. He always saw through my schemes.

A high–pitched voice rose from below.

"Boy, why isn't my saddle properly polished? I should be able to see myself in it."

Lovely. It was my least favorite palace prat, Squire Bertram. I peeked down into the barn and saw just what I expected to see.

Bertie boy and two of his lackeys had my hero backed into a corner. Poor Tim, the stable boy, tried to hide the practice sword, which I'd brought to make him feel more heroic, behind his back. What was Tim's problem? Why didn't he use the practice sword to whack Bertie and his bully boys?

"I– I'm sorry, sir," Tim stammered. "I t–tried to shine your saddle b–but something c–came up."

"Oh, well, that's different, boy. I mean if *something came up...*" Bertie smiled and clapped Tim on the shoulder. "Hey, is that a practice sword you've got there, Tim?"

Tim nodded, knowing what was coming next.

"That's wonderful, Tim! I guess this means you'll be joining us squires at sword training soon!" Bertied grinned over his shoulder at his followers. "You know, I've just had a great idea! Why don't I start your training right now, Tim?"

"N–no, sir, I've got to f–finish p–polishing your saddle."

Bertie lost his false look of congeniality. "It's a little late for that, *boy.*"

My temper flared and I jumped from the loft into a pile of straw behind Bertie and his friends.

"That's enough of that, you stupid bullies!"

Bertie whirled, his face red with anger. "Milk maid, you will regret interfering with your betters!"

Bertie's eyes went wide when he realized who I was. His face paling, the stupid squire dropped to one knee. His bully boys quickly followed suit.

"A thousand pardons, Your Highness! I did not realize it was you who had spoken."

Bertie cringed and bowed even lower. This was more like it!

"You have offended me, Squire Bertram. I order you and your little friends to go run around the palace from now until dinner time."

"But Your Highness, dinner is not for another two hours!"

"Do you think I need you to tell me the time?" I did, actually. I thought dinner was three hours away. Oh well...

"Of course not. I beg your pardon, yet again, for my temerity, Princess Callan."

I cast my best look of disgust upon Bertie and his boys and waved a hand toward the stable doors. "Begone from my sight at once!"

The three squires bowed their heads in acknowledgement and then beat a hasty retreat from the barn.

"Ha! Look at them run!" I grinned in triumph. "You're safe from them now, Tim."

"Don't be foolish, Your Highness. They'll simply come back after you're gone. And the beating Tim receives will be much the worse after he witnessed the way you treated those louts."

It was my turn to cringe, for Tim had not spoken.

I spun about. "Rob, it's not my fault! I–"

"Of course it's your fault, my Princess. *You* took Tim away from his duties. *You* gave him the practice sword. *You* embarrassed the sons of nobles before a defenseless stableboy."

"Don't be silly, Rob! I saved Tim *from* a beating. Tell him, Tim."

"Her Highness is right, of course, Sir Robbill," Tim mumbled.

"See, Rob? Tim admits it!"

"What do you expect him to do, Princess? You just *ordered* him to support your claim."

I rolled my eyes. Rob was being *so* unreasonable!

"Don't be daft, Rob, I'm–"

"The princess and heir to the throne. And as such, your words have power. To someone of Tim's station, your least comment can destroy his life, which is exactly what you have done today." Rob turned to Tim. "Go and gather your things, lad. It's no longer safe for you to work in the stables."

"B–but, sir, I love working here! I knows all the animals and they knows me. Who will mix water in Molly's oats so her old teeth can chew them okay? And nobody 'cept me knows the right place to scritch the king's charger after a hard ride."

"They're not your concern any more, Tim. I'm sorry. I'll do my best to find a similar position for you somewhere else."

Tears spilled down Tim's cheeks as he stumbled away to do Rob's bidding. I felt one tear roll down my cheek, too.

"I didn't mean to do it, Rob," I whispered. "I was just trying to find my hero."

"I know, Little One." Rob put an arm around my shoulder. "But, as I've told you a hundred times, you never find a hero if you go looking for him. But when you least expect it and most need it, a hero will rise to the occasion."

"But what kind of man will that hero be, Rob?"

"God only knows, Your Highness, but, if the hero must save *you*, then I pray the Lord sends us a man of strong will and stronger character!"

I punched Rob's arm, but my heart wasn't in it. I felt badly for what I had done to Tim. And, as I heard Bertie and his bullies run past, I fervently hoped my hero wouldn't turn out to be someone like them.

# Chapter 13

*Callan*

We made good time crossing the desert. Despite the sixteen hour head start enjoyed by the Envoy's ship, the speedy little *Pauline* docked a mere four hours behind the Envoy. Milo slipped into the crowd around the dock, searching for any information concerning David, the tunnel rats, and the plans King Rat had for David.

"You don't speak the language of the city–states, do you, Milo?"

Milo just shook his head as he checked his inventory of...of whatever it was street thieves carried, I guess.

"Then how can your plan succeed if you cannot understand what these people are saying?"

Milo rolled his eyes. What is it about teenagers and eye–rolling? I recall doing it a lot myself—Mom said daughters are particularly prone to it. I'm only twenty–one, but I cannot remember why I thought it was such an effective response to questions from adults. David said it was due to something he called hormones.

"I grew up in a shipping center, Callan," Milo said. "Airships from all over the world docked in Faroon. That meant the docks were filled with tempting targets for thieves. I had to be able to understand bits of a whole bunch of languages if I wanted to find the richest, easiest targets."

"That makes sense, I guess."

Milo flashed his infectious grin and turned away. I pulled him back around and looked into his eyes.

"Be careful and don't do anything careless! You know how David would feel if something happened to you during our rescue attempt!"

Milo rolled his eyes again. "Yes, mother."

Playing along, I planted a kiss on Milo's forehead. "Be a good little boy in the big city! Look both ways when you cross the street and don't talk to any strangers."

The boy rolled his eyes a third time, but he laughed, too.

Two very long hours passed, each of them feeling more like a full day, before Milo returned. His information was worth the time we had spent waiting and I had spent worrying. David had been taken from the Envoy's airship and paraded straight to the lair of the rat king. It was such an unusual procession that it was still the main topic of conversation among those who saw him pass.

"He was walking on his own and nobody said anything about cuts or bruises or bandages. So the envoy must have treated David okay during the trip," Milo wrapped up his report.

"Did anyone notice you while you were out there, Milo? Or follow you back here?" Martin asked.

Milo crossed his arms and glared at Martin.

Martin crossed his arms and glared back. "I had to ask, lad."

"No you didn't."

I rolled *my* eyes. "Now that we've resolved the pressing issue of who had to ask and who didn't, can we get back to rescuing David?"

"Of course, Your Highness. And good job, Milo," Martin said. "Now, I want you to show me where the envoy took David to turn him over to King Rat's men. Along the way, I'll point out a few good bolt holes and some spots where you can land the *Pauline* if the airship has to cut and run while some of us aren't on board."

The man and the boy descended from our dock to the ground. They were quickly absorbed into the crowds teeming around the dock. That left Tristan, Nist, and me to wait and worry. Hiding my identity under the robes and veil of a desert tribeswoman, I paced around the *Pauline's* deck.

Inaction and worry drove my mind into dark places where it delighted in summoning disturbing images. I envisioned tunnel rats killing David in unspeakable ways. Next, what I saw was David and Martin being fed to a tammar. Worst of all, from my mind's darkest corners came the image of Martin turning all of us over to the tunnel rats and keeping the crown jewels for himself. I didn't believe those last images for one second, positive Martin's turn of heart was genuine and his loyalty to David unquestionable. But minds can be insidious and my confidence in Martin didn't stop mine from conjuring those terrible images.

Driven to distraction by my dark thoughts, I wished for something—anything—to happen and grant me relief from the monotony! There is a reason the phrase 'Be careful what you wish for' became a cliché. As if on cue, I spotted Milo dodging through the crowded docks at a run. A gang of burly men pushed through the crowd behind him, losing ground as Milo slipped easily through the crowd.

"Nist! Tristan!" I called. "Milo is coming back here at a run and it looks like he's got an unwelcoming party behind him!"

Milo burst from the mass of people and charged up the stairs to our dock. As he came close enough to be heard over the din of the crowd, he shouted, "Cast off! Cast off!"

Tristan and I ran to do as Milo instructed while Nist tossed a few more logs into the boiler. Nist had insisted on keeping the boiler pressure up—not that any of us had argued with him—and it proved to be a wise move! The gang of men had just reached the bottom of the stairs to our dock when Milo jumped onto the airship. The *Pauline* was fifteen feet above the dock and rising by the time the men reached the top of the stairs. I was relieved to see that they carried small clubs instead of crossbows. They could do nothing more than curse and shake their fists at us.

I fully expected our little drama to have attracted some attention—at home, the dock watch or the city guard would have come swarming in response to behavior like this—but no one gave us a second glance. Maybe foreign dockyards really were as rough and tumble as they were in the air pirate tales I'd read as a girl.

"Why were they chasing you, Milo?" I asked.

"They weren't chasing me, I was racing against them.

"What?"

"Word is out on the streets that Martin stole the Mordanian crown jewels. An awful lot of people know Martin went to visit the tunnel rats. Some of them are hoping to grab the jewels while he's down there. I overheard those thugs say something about 'Bane's airship' and knew that couldn't be good. Their boss must think Martin left the jewels here," Milo said. Pointing behind us, he added, "And that boss isn't going to give up easily!"

Two large airships rose from the docks and swung into our wake!

# Chapter 14

*David*

I watched for a signal from Martin, any kind of signal. I had no idea what his plan was, but I had a pretty good guess what was going on. I hadn't been a guest of King Rat for long, meaning Callan went straight from seeing me off to talking Martin into coming to bring me back. Knowing Martin, she hadn't had to twist his arm.

King Rat waved his hand at me. "As you can see, he is unharmed. And he will stay that way until my preparations are complete."

The head rat spoke in the language of the city–states, which I was not supposed to understand. I cocked my head and adopted a puzzled expression.

"That last bit sounds rather ominous, King Rat. Dare I ask, preparations for what?" Martin also spoke in the local language.

"I have plans for the young man; big, bold, bloody plans. He will be the main attraction at an upcoming celebration, one which will prove fatal to *all* of the attractions, great and small," King Rat replied. "Now, Bane, why are you here and why do you believe I will profit greatly from your visit?"

"I would like to buy David from you," Martin said.

"I told you I have big plans for him," King Rat said. "Why do you think I would have any interest in selling him?"

"Because I'm offering the Mordanian crown jewels," Martin said. "They're yours in return for the lad. Less a small finder's fee, of course. Say, ten percent? It's a win all around, Your Majesty."

"Ah, so the rumors are true. You have reverted to your piratical ways," said King Rat. "That explains the Mordanian naval squadron patrolling a few miles outside of the city."

"Yes, it does. It's a good thing I had a fast airship or they'd have caught me before I reached the safety of Beloren," Martin said. "As for returning to my old profession, let's just say I could not bear to leave such valuable and poorly guarded jewels hidden away in an underground room—especially when those jewels could serve a higher purpose."

"Besides making you rich, you mean."

"That is but a happy side effect, King Rat."

"So, you stole the jewels and flew out of Mordan with the royal navy in your wake. I understand that. What I don't comprehend is why you came to me?"

"It was my plan to slip away unnoticed, unload the crown jewels at a cut rate, and then return to my new life with none the wiser. Alas, my theft was discovered while I was still within Morda's walls. I did only what any prudent thief does—I ran for it," Martin said. "Royalty tends to get more than a tad touchy when it comes to their crown jewels, so touchy that I doubt they'll ever stop hunting for me. On the other hand, I know Her Highness will happily trade the crown jewels to get David back. Since she has the king wrapped around her little finger, if I show up with her husband in tow I'll get a hero's welcome instead of a hangman's noose. You get rich. I get...less rich. And Morda gets their favorite son–in–law back. Have we an agreement?"

"I do believe you're slipping, Bane. Why should I accept *most* of the crown jewels when I can simply take *all* of them from you?" With a languid wave of his hand, a dozen armed men materialized out of the surrounding shadows. "An hour ago, I received a messenger bird from my spies in Morda. They sent word of your act of thievery and provided a quite accurate description of your airship. As we speak, my men are on their way to take the crown jewels from your ship. No one will dare oppose me after I feed an exiled prince, a princess's consort, and the king of the raiders to my new tammar!"

King Rat's harsh laughter echoed through the tunnels as Martin and I were taken to the cell I shared with Raoul.

# Chapter 15

*Callan*

Each of the airships chasing us was three times the size of the *Pauline.* My gaze raked the deck of one of the pursuers. Men crowded the rails, all of them armed with some kind of club or blade. Worse, instead of dwindling behind us, I watched the hulking airships grow larger.

"Nist," I called, "our pursuers are gaining on us. I thought the *Pauline* was the fastest airship around."

"That she is, Your Highness. She is *much* faster than those behemoths. Alas, my girl cannot kick up her keel and really run until we build a bit more boiler pressure," Nist responded. "Milo, please go below and feed the fire!"

Without a word, Milo scampered below. Nist scanned the air ahead of us, his eyes never still for more than a second. Without hesitation, Nist turned the *Pauline* toward the crowded space above the center of the dock. Airships of all shapes and sizes twisted and turned across our path, forming a living maze of rope and wood and gas envelopes

"What are you doing, Nist?" I cried. "All that traffic will do is slow us down!"

"Indeed it will, Your Highness. But the *Pauline* is small and nimble. I can fly through it," Nist replied. "But those great tubs chasing us will have no chance of keeping up with us inside that tangle of airships. If they try to follow us, we'll be long gone before they can ever get clear. If they go around, it will give our boiler pressure time to rise."

Tearing my eyes off of the swirling mass of ships before us, I looked back at our pursuers. Nist was right. One airship swung ponderously to starboard, flying around the knot of traffic. The other ship went to port, giving the ships their best chance of catching us when we got clear of the other airships.

Nist's hands flew over the *Pauline's* controls, guiding our little ship in and out of the much larger ships around us. Shouts and curses rose in our wake as the *Pauline* skimmed so close to some ships that I could have reached out and touched them.

Tristan approached me. "Highness, Nist has bought us a little breathing space with this move. It would be wise to use that time to plan our course once we're free of these other airships."

"You're right, of course." Tristan should not have had to remind me. I had let myself get caught up in the excitement of the moment. "Do we even have a choice? Our safest course will be to head for the Mordanian naval squadron north of the city."

"That would be the safest course for *us*, Your Highness," Tristan said.

"But?"

"Is that the course a raider crew would choose? Tristan said. "Especially a crew who had, supposedly, been chased across the desert by that same squadron?"

I smacked myself on the forehead. "No, of course not. What was I thinking?"

I had been thinking like a princess, and that was a real problem. Mistakes like that would get my husband and Martin killed! With David at the forefront of my mind, I forced myself away from proper princess thinking. It was time to start thinking and acting like a criminal!

But what would a raider crew do in this situation? Approached from that point of view, the answer was simple—they'd do whatever it took to get away from the airships chasing them while also avoiding the Mordanian naval squadron.

"Tell Nist to set whatever course he thinks is best for both escaping our pursuers *and* steering clear of the naval squadron," I said. "I trust his judgement."

Tristan grinned. "An excellent idea, Highness. Do you have any idea what we'll do after we get away?"

"I haven't got a clue, Tristan," I replied. "But that doesn't concern me at all. If I haven't figured out what we're doing next, you can bet our enemies will be in deeper darkness than we will."

As Tristan relayed my command to Nist, I smiled to myself. Tristan had said exactly what I had needed to hear. By letting myself get so wrapped up making plans, I had abandoned my one real strength. It was time to stop planning and start reacting.

*"Good instincts are nothing more than your brain working at top speed. Your subconscious mind analyzes situations faster than your conscious mind,"* Rob had told me. *"Go with your gut, Your Highness. It will serve you well."*

A minute later, we flew clear of the worst of the dockyard traffic. At the same time, our pursuers rounded the knot of airships and closed in on our path from both sides. Nist opened the throttle and the *Pauline* drove toward the narrowing gap between the airships!

# Chapter 16

*David*

Six guards escorted Martin and me to the cell I shared with Raoul. The guards took yet another circuitous route from the throne room to the dungeon. If nothing else, I had the beginnings of an excellent map of the inhabited part of the tunnels.

At any time during the walk, Martin and I could have taken the six tunnel rats with little trouble. The guards had never seen either of us Boost. They would be counting on their swords and superior numbers, neither of which would be anywhere near as useful against the two of us as they thought. But escape was not my plan—at least, not yet. And either Martin was waiting for me to make the first move or escape wasn't his immediate plan, either.

He did, however, play the part of a wronged visiting dignitary with convincing outrage.

"I demand to be taken back to King Rat this instant! Before entering this wretched warren of tunnels, I arranged for safe passage to meet with him. I insist he honor that safe passage!"

One of the guards smacked Martin's back with the flat of his blade. "Watch your tongue, raider! King Rat always honors his deals. You wanted safe passage *to* His Majesty. You got to your meeting safe and sound. Your deal didn't say nothing about safe passage *away* from him!"

"It most certainly *did* include safe passage out of these tunnels. I was not born yesterday!"

"Like I said, raider, King Rat *mostly* honors his deals."

The guards all laughed at this display of tunnel rat humor.

"This is outrageous!" Martin actually sputtered as he spoke. It was an impressive performance. "I am not some low-life beggar to be treated as King Rat pleases! I am—"

"Going to get in that cell and shut up," the guard said. For emphasis, he prodded Martin with the tip of his sword.

The guards chained Martin and me to the same wall. When the cell door swung shut, blocking the guards' torch, we were cast into absolute darkness again. Through the door, we heard the guards laughing and mimicking Martin's outrage as they walked away.

"Well, that was an unexpected development," Martin said. "Still, I suppose matters could be worse."

"Who's that?" Raoul's sleepy voice came from the darkness. "Rice? Are you back?"

"Yes, Raoul, I'm back."

"*Raoul?*" Martin asked.

"Bane? You came to save me, too?" Raoul's voice cracked with emotion.

"David, why does Raoul think I'm here to rescue him?"

"He thinks I'm here for the same reason. Raoul's been down here a long time, at least a couple of months." I shrugged, then realized no one could see it. "I think the darkness and isolation have affected his perception of reality. Knowing Raoul, he's probably got crazy voices in his head telling him we're here for him."

"Doesn't that just beat all?" Martin said. "Still, I suppose you could call his presence a good omen."

"Having Raoul inflicted on us is good? This must be some new and hitherto unknown definition of that word."

"David, surely you watched enough old adventure vids to know you can't have a dungeon escape without some crazy prisoner tagging along for comic relief."

"Ha! So you *are* here to rescue me!"

"Shut up, Raoul," Martin and I said in unison.

"I watched a lot of adventure vids, Martin. Isn't the crazy prisoner supposed to know some secret the hero can use to emerge triumphant?"

"Okay, our situation isn't an exact match with the vids. But that was the best spin I could put on Raoul's presence on such short notice." Chains clinked in the darkness as Martin changed positions. "Why didn't we jump the guards on the trip down here, David?"

"I want our escape to be more awe inspiring. I can't just clear out of here, I've got to make sure King Rat can never terrorize the city-states into doing his bidding again."

"Okay, I can see the sense in that idea. What's your plan?"

"Plan isn't really the word I'd use for it. It's more of a scheme..."

# Chapter 17

*Callan*

Traffic thinned around us and Nist angled the bow of the *Pauline* up. The two ships angled their bows up as well. Just as quickly, Nist dropped the bow of our ship, angling down toward the city below. The pursuer to port angled down while the ship to starboard didn't alter its course. They had our path covered regardless of what angle Nist took. But how were they communicating over such distances?

My gaze was caught by flashes of movement from the ships. Men waved flags on the decks of both of the airships. They must have signals to coordinate their actions. Now that they had our likely paths covered, I wondered what else they might be signaling. *Fly faster, me fine lads!* It sounded like a line from an air pirate story, so probably not. *Dibs on the girl in the veil!* That sounded like a line from an air pirate story, too, but it still sent a shiver down my spine! I decided it would be best to stop thinking about the signals.

"Nist," I called, "are we going to get past those airships before they can cut us off?"

Nist eyed the closing airships for a second or two then shook his head. "No, Your– um, I mean, no ma'am."

"Back in my room at the palace, I told you I needed a daring pilot, Nist." I tore my gaze from the converging airships and looked at Nist. "So please tell me you've got a daring plan to elude those ships and get us out of the city."

"Of course he does, Callan." Tristan's voice boomed heartily, an adventurous twinkle lighting his eyes. "After all, I taught the lad everything he knows!"

"We're all going to die!" cried Milo, emerging onto the deck after stoking the boiler.

Tristan struggled to keep a straight face. I laughed, amazed anew at the courage and wit of my companions.

"I do have a plan to get away from those ships and daring doesn't even begin to describe it," Nist said over my laughter. "You should all hold on to something."

I caught one of the stays with one hand and gave a mock salute with the other. "Aye aye, sir!"

"You'll want to use two hands, ma'am." Nist never took his eyes from the other two airships.

A smile played across Nist's face as his hands flew over the *Pauline's* controls. My pilot's face had the faraway look I knew meant he was about to do something that bordered on foolhardy. I grabbed the stay with both hands and then wrapped one leg around it for good measure. A quick look aft showed that Milo and Tristan had done the same.

Our pursuers had changed their courses again, with one ship coming up from below us and the other coming down from above us. The flags no longer flashed and crewmen lined the rails of both ships. We were so close I could see individual crewmen clearly. One scratched his nose. Another leered at me with a toothless grin.

"Nist? Shouldn't you be doing something?" I tried to keep my voice level, but even I could hear the rising note at the end.

"Almost, ma'am." Nist adjusted the ailerons and braced himself. "*Now!*"

He spun the wheel hard to port with one hand and worked the ailerons with the other. The *Pauline* swung up so sharply our keel brushed the rigging of one of our pursuers! I heard cries as some of the other ship's airmen were knocked from their perches in that rigging. The remaining crews of the pursuing airships gaped as Nist leveled the *Pauline* and shoved the throttle wide open. With a roar, our ship surged away from the two ships. Too late, the captains of those ships remembered their courses. In a chorus of cries from the crews, the twang of taut rope snapping, and the crash of splintering wood, the two ships smashed into each other.

My heart raced, adrenaline surged through my veins, and the whole world seemed sharper and more alive. Was this what David felt when he Boosted? I struggled to hold onto the feeling, but it faded as quickly as it had begun.

Milo was the first to regain his voice. "That. Was. *Amazing!*"
Free of pursuit, we sped toward the edge of the city.

# Interlude

*David is Thirteen*

I pulled my pad out of my pocket and answered the vid call.

"Hi, Art. What's up?"

"A bunch of us are going over to Steve's to play some games. He got the new Virt Box for his birthday and he says it's fusing fantastic."

That sounded great, more than great, but I shook my head.

"I wish I could, but I'm going over to Mr. Hart's. I've got to help him with a few chores, stuff he can't do on his own any more."

Art rolled his eyes. "Is he going to tell you more of his stupid stories?"

"You didn't use to think Mr. Hart's stories were stupid."

"Yeah, when I was *seven*. Then I grew up and realized Mr. Hart just made all that stuff up."

"I think there's some real truth behind the stories. But even if he *did* make them up, we all loved listening to them." I paused for a second. "You know, he asks about all of you whenever I visit. It would make him real happy if you guys came with me."

Art held up his hands as if they were old fashioned measuring scales and looked back and forth between the hands.

"New Virt Box or old man's stories."

He repeated that several times, moving his hands up and down each time. Then he brought one hand up and left it there. "Virt Box. Sorry, David, stories lose."

"Yeah, whatever."

I thumbed the call off, pocketed my pad, and headed for the door.

"Where are you off to, David?" Mom called.

"I told Mr. Hart I'd come by and help him do some stuff around the house."

"You just want him to tell you more stories so you can dream about meeting a spacebabe of your own!"

Why are little sisters so annoying?

"Shut up, brat!"

"Sandra, don't tease your brother. David, don't talk to your sister like that." Mom glared for a second to drive home the point, then she smiled at me. "I'm proud of you for sticking by Mr. Hart, son. I know it means a lot to him, too. Dinner's at seven."

Walking across the street, I couldn't help but turn my gaze to the clear, blue sky. Two of the moons hung in the sky, visible reminders of all that lay out there, beyond the sky. Whether Mr. Hart's stories were true or not, he had been into space. He'd walked on other worlds. Even if he'd never met a spacebabe, he was living proof that the galaxy still had room for adventures.

*That* was the real reason I liked visiting with him. I still thought his stories were fun, but just knowing Mr. Hart had done all of that real stuff gave me hope that I could do something extraordinary with my life, too.

He answered the door before the bell had stopped chiming. He craned his neck a bit, looking to see if anyone else was with me.

"None of the other boys wanted to come along?"

His broad smile never wavered, but his eyes dimmed a bit.

"They're all studying for a big test in school tomorrow." The lie came easily, just like the other lies I told when he asked why no one else came to visit.

"Well, shouldn't you be studying, too, David?"

"Nah, I've got that stuff down cold, Mr. Hart."

"You always were a smart boy." He backed up a couple of steps. "Well, come on in and let's get started on those chores. I don't want to keep you."

"There's no rush, sir. I'll stick around as long as you need me to help out." I gave Mr. Hart a smile. "And, as long as I live across the street, I always will."

# Chapter 18

*David*

"*That* is your plan?" Martin asked.

I couldn't see him in the darkness but imagined him shaking his head in dismay.

"No, that's my *scheme*. There's a reason I told you I wouldn't go so far as to call it a plan!"

"I like it!" Raoul sounded chipper. We must have been more entertaining than the voices in his head. "I especially like the part where you kill the King Rat for mistreating me so badly!"

"There, if Raoul likes the plan it can't possibly succeed!" Martin said.

"If you've got a better plan, I'm all ears," I said.

Martin was silent for a while then asked, "What makes you think it'll work?"

"The tunnel rats don't know about Boost," I said.

"So we Boost, jump the guards, take their weapons, and disappear into the tunnels," Martin said. "Then we make a few hit-and-fade raids and watch for a chance to take out King Rat. But what do we do with Raoul?"

"We take him with us," I sighed. "Not even Raoul deserves to be eaten alive by a tammar. Besides, he'll warn the guards if we don't take him."

"And I can fight with you!" Raoul added.

"Only if we're truly desperate," Martin said. "I guess we'd better get started. You want to go first or should I?"

"It's my idea, so I ought to be the one to try it first."

I stood up, wrapping links of the chain about my arm and wrist. In the light of the guards' lantern, the chain had looked old and badly rusted, as did the bolts holding the chain to the wall. I put my right foot against the wall next to the bolts.

*Boost!*

As adrenaline flooded my system, I threw my weight and all of my Boosted strength into pulling the chain from the wall. I thought I felt the chain give a bit and really wished I could see what effect I was having. Then I brought my left foot against the wall, as well, keeping myself up solely through the force I exerted against the wall.

With a shriek of tortured metal, the chain stretched and broke. I had just enough time to tuck into a ball before I hit the floor and rolled into the far wall. I dropped Boost.

"Ow."

"Good job, lad! I trust nothing is broken other than the chain?"

"Just a few scrapes and bruises. Your turn, old man."

A moment later, Martin crashed into the wall next to me.

"Ow, indeed. At least we're free."

"Which one of you is going to break my chain?"

"We're not breaking your chain, Raoul."

"But David said you were going to take me with you!"

"Yes, I said that—and I meant it. But we're just going to unlock your chains with the key we take from the guards."

A sigh sounded in the darkness. "Oh."

Martin and I went back to our positions against the other wall, our chains balled up around one fist. Then we had nothing else to do but wait for the guards to return.

Scouts spend a lot of time traveling through space alone. A lot of our training centered around staving off boredom and remaining alert during long periods of inactivity. I'd never been very good at it and was even worse in the current situation. I was relieved beyond imagining when I finally heard the echo of approaching footsteps. A moment later, dim light shone along the bottom of the door. Metal scraped on metal as a key was inserted into the lock. We heard a click as the key turned.

Seven men—more than I was expecting—stepped into the room. One balanced three bowls on a tray. The other six held swords. In the dim light, I gave a nod to Martin.

*Boost!*

# Chapter 19

*Callan*

Our pursuers' ships spun around each other, each entangled in the other ship's rigging. Men who hungrily eyed our airship mere seconds ago reeled and tumbled across their decks. Some rolled over the railing, plunging to their death far below. Nearby ships climbed, dove, and turned to avoid being caught in the wreck. Those sudden maneuvers made ships farther from the gyrating wreck dodge and dive.

Like the ripple from a pebble dropped in a pool, chaos spread throughout the skies above the dock. Airships from the city watch, conspicuous by their absence a moment ago, finally put in an appearance, steaming into the maelstrom to investigate the situation. For the first time ever, the Beloren city watch proved helpful to me. Refusing to yield their path to other ships, the watch airships added to the confusion and further helped cover our escape.

"Nist, that was the most fun ever!" Milo wore the widest grin I'd seen on his face since he'd kissed his first young lady-in-waiting at the palace. "Let's do it again!"

"I most strenuously insist we *not* do that again! Once was quite enough, young man," Tristan said. "I'm sure that little stunt shaved weeks off my remaining life!"

"Her High- The lady did ask for a *daring* escape plan," Nist said, "not a staid old man escape plan!"

"Never let it be said you don't give a girl what she asks for!" I said. "I'll have to warn Kim about that when we get back home."

Even that mild jest caused scarlet blooms on Nist's cheeks. Daring pilot? Definitely yes. Clueless lover? Emphatically yes. Coaxing first moves out of Nist would require the help of an expert. I'd better talk to Mom when we got back. With her advising Kim, Nist would never know what hit him!

As we flew over what was left of the Beloren southern city wall, Nist asked, "What course should I set, ma'am?"

"Nist, please stop calling me *ma'am*," I said. "You're making me feel old. I'm younger than you are!"

"I will try...Callan," Nist said.

"That's better. As for a course..." I turned to Tristan. "Tristan, how far is it to the nearest desert tribe camp?"

"The tribes are nomadic people, lass. They rarely stay in place for more than a few months." Tristan shrugged. "I know of four tribes who usually stay within a few hours flight of Beloren. They all leave signs so other tribes can find them. You just have to know what to look for."

"Please tell me you know the signs," I implored.

"Oh, aye. I'm not called the Desert Doctor for nothing, my dear," Tristan said. "Are you planning to hide out with a tribe for a day or two?"

"No," I said, "I'm going to ask them for directions."

"It's a desert, Callan," Nist said. "What are you going to ask directions *to*?"

With more confidence than I felt, I said, "The nearest trog settlement!"

# Chapter 20

*David*

My implant flooded my system with adrenaline. The guards seemed to slow, their actions and reactions telegraphed far in advance. Our speed disrupted what little group cohesion the guards had, leaving them attacking empty air or even each other.

Only Martin moved at what was, to me, normal speed. We had no need to communicate or coordinate our actions. For decades, Scout Academy training covered tandem fighting under Boost. No cadet graduated without first mastering this skill. As long as each scout knew his role, coordination was assured.

It was my mission. It was my plan. It was my lead.

Surging past the man bringing our food, I grabbed his collar and flung him backward and into the guards gathered just inside the door. My chain-wrapped fist caught the closest guard with an uppercut, lifting him off his feet and loosening his grip on his sword. I snatched the loose sword in midair and used it to block an attack from another guard. I ducked a thrust from a third guard and then ran him through. Then the second guard was back. I batted his wild swing aside, catching the blade with the chain, then slashed him with the sword. Blood spurted from his shoulder as I cut it to the bone. His sword clattered to the floor and I smashed him on the head with my chain-wrapped fist.

As the second guard collapsed in a bloody heap, the first guard grabbed his fallen sword. Diving across the floor, he lunged for my legs. I skipped over the attack then stepped on the blade, pinning it to floor. As the guard tried to roll away, I kicked him in the head. He sprawled limp on the floor, down for the count.

I checked on Martin. He drew his sword from the belly of the last guard standing and the man sagged to the floor. In the sudden silence, I heard the receding footsteps of the man who'd carried the food tray.

We dropped Boost.

"Should we chase after the runner?" Martin asked.

"No. Better King Rat hears of the fight from an eye witness. The tale the servant babbles to the rat king will be incoherent and, most likely, exaggerated. King Rat won't believe half of it, but his people will."

I grabbed a ring of keys from one of the guards and removed the manacles from Martin's wrist and mine. Kneeling next to Raoul, I freed him as well.

"Get up, Spare Prince. It's time to get out of here."

"Let me grab a sword–" Raoul began.

"No!" I said. "No sword until you prove we can trust you."

Grabbing the guards' lantern, I led our little band into the darkness!

# Chapter 21

*Callan*


A moment of silence followed my announcement.

"Lass..." Tristan stretched the word out, as if searching for the best way to approach a delicate subject. "Why do you want to find a trog settlement? Except for attacks of retribution, I've never heard of humans searching for trog settlements."

"After our narrow escape from Beloren, I believe it's safe to say Martin's plan to buy David back didn't work."

Tristan nodded in agreement.

"We had no expectations it would, but we *did* expect Martin to come back to us. So we must assume Martin is also King Rat's prisoner, perhaps even sharing a cell with David."

"I suspect you're right on all accounts, my dear." Tristan spoke slowly, as if trying to calm down an emotional woman. Did he think I was about to get hysterical? "But that doesn't explain why you want to find trogs?"

"I doubt King Rat has a cell that can hold David against his will. That goes double if Martin is with him. But you know how David behaves when he's being noble. He won't even consider an escape from King Rat if he believes it will lead to the very war he stopped by surrendering to the envoy." I watched dawning comprehension in Tristan's eyes. "If I want to see my husband again, I need to go into those tunnels and fetch him. If I want to survive that trip, I'll need warriors."

"I see your point, Callan, but I don't believe you've thought this through." Tristan was still speaking slowly and it was getting on my nerves. "We have a Mordanian naval squadron only a few miles from here, one tasked by your mother to protect and aid you. Surely Mordanian marines would be a better choice than a bunch of trogs!"

"My oh my, Tristan, why ever did I not think of that?" Tristan's eyebrows shot up at my tone. I guess he wasn't used to being on the

160

receiving end of such deep sarcasm. "Yes, those marines would be just perfect for the job!"

I got into Tristan's face, channeling Rob when he dressed down a young guardsman. "If the job was to start a war with Beloren and her allied city-states! Something David went to extreme measures to avoid."

"Well... Yes. Um, I see your point!" Tristan fell back a step.

"Good. I'm not some love-crazed young woman risking everything just to save her man!" I turned to Nist. "Swing around the city and fly past the squadron. Get close enough for them to identify us but not so close that they can hail us. Discreetly raise my flag during the fly-by so they'll know I'm on board. I expect they'll follow us."

I looked at Tristan. "If there are no other objections...?"

"No! None here, lass. None at all."

I flashed my best good-girl smile. "I didn't think so. Now, let's go find those trogs!"

# Chapter 22

*David*

The light from the guards' lantern provided weak illumination as we forged into the dark tunnels of King Rat's domain. My implant recorded every twist and turn we took, expanding the map I began recording when the tunnel rats led me to the dungeon. Martin's implant recorded our progress, as well. We had to learn these tunnels so well we could navigate them in pitch darkness or if one of us was out on his own.

The beginnings of a plan took shape in my mind, but for it to succeed we had to know the tunnels better than the tunnel rats knew them. It was an impossible task made entirely possible by our implants. King Rat counted the maze of dark tunnels as his first line of defense. We would make it the front line of our offense.

For hours, we skirted the edges of tunnel rat territory. As the lantern oil burned down, we replenished our supply from wall lanterns just within the sections used by the tunnel rats. A picture of King Rat's underground empire emerged from our explorations. I expected to find squalor and filth, a sad existence for a pathetic band of ragged beggars and thieves, forced to eat rats and drink dirty water in order to survive. With the exception of an elite few, I expected disease-ridden savages barely scraping by under their king's iron rule.

Reality dashed my fantasy into little bits and then stomped all over the bits. We found a large and well organized food supply, complete with barrels of fresh water and freshly slaughtered meat. Tempting aromas wafted from a huge, bustling kitchen just down the tunnel from the food store. Just past the kitchen we found a vast communal dining area. We stole through the empty dining room to scout what lay beyond it. Room after room furnished for sleeping, with separate quarters for women and men, as well as quarters for families.

The slave quarters were poorly furnished in comparison, but they far exceeded what I had expected to find. We even found a nursery where children stayed while their parents were out and about, doing King Rat's bidding. The children were the real surprise. Innocent childish laughter clashed with my original image of tunnel life. In retrospect, I realize I should not have been surprised. All human cultures reproduce, even the tunnel rats.

We retreated into unused tunnels, our map of King Rat's territory greatly expanded after the hours we spent exploring. The three of us retraced our path to an intersection of tunnels well outside of the populated areas. Torch and lantern light, which we would spot long before anyone came close to us, would offer ample warning if anyone came looking for us. The intersection also provided several lines of retreat, if King Rat sent a large force.

"There are a lot more people down here than I expected," Martin said. "How many do you think are down here?"

A voice whined from the darkness. "Why haven't you gotten me out of these tunnels?"

"Shut up, Raoul," Martin and I said in unison.

"I'd guess there are close to a thousand people, counting children and slaves." A thought occurred to me. "From the size of their quarters, there must be a lot of slaves. Do you think we can count on their support?"

"Maybe a few will support us. As for the rest, it depends on how long they've been down here. Raoul's only been here a couple of months and look at him. I expect most of the slaves have given up hope. When you get around to expanding your scheme into a plan, don't count on support from the slaves."

"You'll be happy to learn my plan doesn't involve the slaves."

"You have an actual plan?" Martin asked. "It's not David's Scheme Mark II?"

"It's an actual plan. I came up with it while we were exploring," I said. "I'd even go as far as to say it's tailor-made for you."

"Uh huh. Tell me the plan and then I'll let you know if I agree with your assessment."

I grinned. "We're going to be raiders!"

# Chapter 23

*David*

Martin approved of my plan. Raoul, on the other hand, did not.

"As a prince of Tarteg, I will not sully my reputation by hoisting the raider flag!"

"Yes, perish the thought, Spare Prince!" Martin's tone dripped sarcasm. "Kidnapping princesses so a prince as pathetic as you can be reborn as a hero is just fine and dandy, though."

"You're forgetting a rather important part of that plan, raider Captain Bane. *You* are the one who kidnapped the princess!" This was more like the Raoul I knew and loathed so well. "I knew nothing of that plan until after the deed was done."

"Yet you went along with the plan when you did learn of it, Raoul. A simple word from you and I'd have released the princess."

"And you could have released the princess at any time, with or without word from me!"

"Both of you, *shut up!*"

"But Bane–"

"Shut. Up."

Raoul locked eyes with me and, in the lantern light, his eyes glowed red. Without another word, he jumped to his feet and charged down the tunnel and into the darkness. Martin and I watched him vanish from sight.

"Shouldn't we go after him, David?"

"Nah. Raoul has no idea where he's going. On the other hand, I know this tunnel turns right about a hundred feet from here." I listened to Raoul's fading footsteps. "He should hit the wall right about...now!"

We heard a thud followed by the sound of a body hitting the floor.

"Okay, *now* we can go after him, Martin."

We rose and ambled down the tunnel.

"Does this mean I can finally slit the little jerk's throat?"

"I'm tempted to let you, Martin, but Callan would never approve."

"I just *knew* you were going to use Callan as a means of depriving me of my fun. Okay, if we're not going to rid the world of Raoul, what are we going to do with him?"

"Something worse than killing him, my friend. We're going to lock him back in the cell."

Raoul regained consciousness as I snapped the chain about his wrist. He screamed and cursed and pleaded and even cried like a baby. Martin and I smiled and waved as we locked the door.

Lighter of heart than we'd felt since ending up in the cell with Raoul, Martin and I planned our first strike.

Along with the implant–aided mental maps of the tunnels, we discovered King Rat kept the rat kingdom on a tight schedule. He had the place running like clockwork, and that made planning our raids all the easier.

We stuck with simple military tactics and raided the kitchen first. It doesn't matter how much people love or fear their leader, any leader who fails to feed his people is in for some serious control problems.

The kitchen staff appeared to have one job, watching the kitchen slaves and beating them if they didn't work hard enough to suit their masters. Martin and I waited until the kitchen staff arrived to start preparing breakfast then made our move.

"Get lost." The kitchen foreman's arm slashed the air, negating the request he expected to hear. "No food until morning."

I kept walking toward him. With a snarl, the foreman raised the wooden staff he used to beat the slaves and swung it at me. I stepped inside the swing, caught the foreman's wrist and twisted. He cried out in pain as bones snapped. I took the staff from the foreman's unresisting hand and broke it over his head. The foreman collapsed, moaning.

The kitchen staff and the slaves stared at Martin and me, too shocked to react. The shock wore off faster than I'd have hoped.

"Slaves, get them!"

With a smack, one of the staff hit a slave on the backside and the slaves shuffled toward us.

*Boost!*

Adrenaline poured into our veins. Time slowed for Martin and me. We brushed aside the half-hearted slave attacks, gently pushing them into a confused jumble. The kitchen staff backpedaled as we waded in among them. Each of them got the same treatment as the foreman. Seconds later, we dropped Boost.

The slaves retreated into a corner when I turned to face them.

"We're here to free you, not hurt you. Will you come with us?"

The slaves exchanged glances and a few shrugs before one spoke.

"We have little choice. They will kill us if we stay."

"Then gather as much cooked food and fresh water as you can carry. You are slaves no longer!"

As the former slaves gathered supplies, Martin and I locked the staff in a cellar. Our next stop was the food store. We put the remaining food to the torch and then led our well-supplied band into the darkness.

We had struck our first blow against King Rat!

# Chapter 24

*Callan*

Nist swung wide of Beloren, just as we'd done months before when the city was aflame. The afternoon sun shone from behind the squadron as we sped past it. Milo hoisted my flag at the closest point of our fly-by. With the early afternoon sunlight streaming in from behind the Mordanian ships, the glare kept us from watching for activity on those decks. Instead, I watched the green and gold colors of my country snapping in the breeze.

"Will their lookouts see the flag, Your Highness?" Milo asked.

"If they don't, my father will demote every last officer on board those ships! And I've told you many times that you may use my first name in private settings like this, Milo."

"Yes, I remember, Your Highness." Milo's infectious grin lit his face. "But, Your Highness, I couldn't do that while we're flying Your Highness's personal flag, Your Highness!"

I crossed my arms and called forth what David calls princess mode. "Then take the flag down this instant, you wretched child! Yonder squadron is raising steam and getting under way."

"Your Highness's wish is my command, Your Highnessness!" Milo folded the flag and gave an innocent smile. "Will there be anything else, Callan?"

I pretended to swat at the boy, he pretended to be scared, and I had a much-needed laugh.

Over the next three hours, Tristan's gaze swept over the desert ahead of the airship, searching for signs of a desert tribe camp. I saw nothing but sand and dunes to the far horizon. Tristan's cries of "Ah ha!" followed by directions called to Nist had me wondering if my eyesight was failing.

"What does Tristan see down there, Callan? All I see is sand. And then I look more closely and I still just see sand. And then, look, more sand!"

"You can search me, Milo."

Milo gave a sly smile. "Really? Don't you think David will object to me doing that?"

What happened to the innocent child I met in Faroon all those months ago?

My tone was drier than the desert below us as I asked, "What do you think? Besides, don't you have a girlfriend back at the palace?"

"Not really, no," Milo muttered.

Behind us, Nist gave a rather bitter laugh. "Milo hoped to have a girlfriend in the palace, Callan. Alas, young Lady Lucile's mother is wary of a street urchin with aspirations above his station."

"She did *not* say that about Milo, did she?"

"Yeah, she did, and right to Kim's face, too."

"Well, Milo, I will have quite a few choice words for *her* when I get back! The very idea of anyone treating a hero of Faroon like that boils my blood!"

"Don't do it, Callan! I've got a reputation to maintain. Having my sort-of big sister rush to my defense won't help it one bit!"

"Sort-of big sister? That's so sweet, Milo! But my mind is made up! The nerve of that woman!" Then I caught sight of the pleading in Milo's eyes and reined in my temper. "Very well, Milo. I won't say anything to Lady Lucile's mother."

Then the answer came to me and I burst out laughing.

"Okay, Callan, what's so funny? You already promised you wouldn't talk to her."

"And I won't, Milo." I rarely get to use my evil princess smile very often, but this occasion called for it. "Instead, I will tell Mother about it."

Milo's evil smile was better than mine and he had a cackling laugh to go with it.

Tristan's voice rose over Milo's cackle. "If you three are finished dishing up court gossip, I require the aid of young eyes over here."

When Milo and I joined him, Tristan pointed off in the distance. "Is that smudge out there just another dune or is it something else?"

I looked past his pointing finger, gasped, and then planted a kiss on his cheek. "It's a camp, Tristan! You did it!"

"It's easy if you know what to look for, my dear."

Ten minutes later, Nist brought the *Pauline* down just outside the camp. Per my orders—orders the squadron commander disliked in the extreme—the squadron stayed aloft and the rails of the airships were *not* teeming with marines.

The tribesmen were no more pleased to have the squadron hovering overhead than the commander was to be stuck up there. The tribal leaders only met with us out of respect for Tristan. In fact, the familiar sight of the *Pauline* was all that kept them from scattering into the desert. At least everyone was equally unhappy, right?

Tristan spoke to the tribal leaders with me standing decorously at his side. The leaders gestured wildly as they spoke and Tristan did the same when he replied. After a few minutes of this, an older tribesman pointed at me, his other arm pointing into the village. Tristan's eyebrows rose and then he responded far more energetically than before. The tribesman gestured to me again and then pointed some more. Tristan and the tribesman went back and forth several times before I got impatient.

"Tristan, this was supposed to be a simple introduction. Why is it taking so long?"

"I'm rather embarrassed to say, Your Highness."

"Get over your embarrassment and tell me what the hold up is."

"The elder wants to...buy you. He's been looking for a wife for his youngest son and you meet with his approval." To my amazement, Tristan blushed. "He believes you'll produce far more attractive children than his elder son's wife."

I faced the tribesman. "I am not for sale."

"I have told him that several times, Your Highness. He thinks I'm haggling and responds by raising his offer." Tristan grinned, his sense of humor returning. "He thinks quite highly of you, my dear. His offer is up to two horses, a herd of goats, *and* a tent."

I fought the urge to laugh, myself. "I'm flattered. Tell him I'm married to a mighty and jealous warrior. Then tell him about David's battles with the trogs. That ought to give the old guy pause."

Tristan chattered and gestured and even thrust an imaginary sword at an imaginary foe.

Excited chatter broke out among the tribesmen after Tristan finished speaking. The hard–bargaining tribesman faced me and bowed low. The rest of the tribal leaders followed his lead.

"Tristan, what's going on?"

Tristan turned a stunned face to me. "They've heard of David. Around here, he's known as the Hand of Death."

"What? Who could have possibly told the tribes about David?"

"That's the part which makes no sense, Your Highness. The desert tribes heard of David from the trogs!"

# Chapter 25

*Callan*

I stared at Tristan, my mouth hanging open in a most unprincess-like manner. I tried to wrap my mind around what Tristan had just told me and simply could not do so.

Seeing I was at a loss for words, Tristan nodded his head toward the tribal leaders. They all still held their bows.

"Oh! Thank you, Tristan. Please tell them to rise."

I regained some of my mental equilibrium as Tristan spoke to the leaders. They rose and faced me with expectant looks.

"Find out how the trogs could tell the tribes anything, much less stories about David. I thought the Great One was the only being—trog or human—who had ever been able to speak the other's language!"

Tristan and the tribesmen spoke for several minutes, gesturing dramatically. It was fascinating, but also frustrating. I *hate* speaking through translators! Conversations take three times as long and even the best translator can make a mistake or miss a vital detail. What I wouldn't have given to have one of those implant things that David had in his head!

Finally, Tristan turned to me. "The story is long, as you no doubt guessed, but here is the short version. Many centuries ago, the growing city-states to the south and expanding kingdoms to the north pushed both the tribes and the trogs into the desert. Enemies of old, the tribes and trogs waged war against each other for many years. Declining populations on both sides led to the realization that their true battle was against the desert. Their shared enemy led the two groups to form a loose alliance of sorts. Your Highness, these people have been trading with the trogs for at least two centuries. Over that time, a fairly sophisticated sign language has evolved between the trogs and the tribes."

"So these tribesmen can ask the trogs where to find the Great One?"

Tristan shrugged. "So they say."

"Do you believe them?"

"Most definitely. I've treated all of these men and their families many times. I have never known them to be anything but honest in their dealings with me."

"Then ask them if we can borrow a translator."

Tristan relayed my request. The tribesman who had tried to buy me responded.

"What did he say?"

"First, he apologizes most profusely for attempting to purchase you."

"Tell him it is forgotten."

"There is no need. I took the liberty of accepting his apology on your behalf." A wicked grin creased Tristan's face, "Further more, as a token of their respect and admiration for the Hand of Death, he hopes Lady Death will accept the services of their best translator."

"Lady Death? You're making that up, Tristan!"

"I swear on all I hold sacred that I am not! What else should they call the wife of the Hand of Death?"

There was a phrase which described the grin Tristan gave me. When I was much younger, my mother had assured me it was not something proper princesses said.

"Could you at least *pretend* you're not enjoying this so much?" I asked. "Accept their generous offer and get this translator on board the *Pauline*. We leave in ten minutes."

Tristan swept into a bow. "As m'Lady Death commands!"

Ten minutes later, the translator came aboard and the *Pauline* rose to join the naval squadron. We were one step closer to the trogs and to rescuing David!

# Chapter 26

*David*

Everything went as planned—better, since we only saw Raoul long enough to give him food and water and make certain he remained securely chained in the cell. The Spare Prince expressed his displeasure every time we visited, but even he was smart enough to keep his voice down. King Rat struck no one as an 'enemy of my enemy is my friend' type of person.

On our first visit, Raoul blustered and threatened. In a weird way, I was relieved to hear him rant like that. It meant Raoul was getting back to his usual, irritating self. Even that odious personality was better than the mewling shell of a man I'd originally found in the cell.

The next time we visited, he demanded his freedom a second time. Again, it was to no avail.

Meanwhile, our kitchen raid had achieved its purpose. King Rat's people were hungry and disorganized. The king tried to anticipate our next move and laid a trap for us at the armory. We hit his store of lantern oil and torches, instead. In the aftermath, the tunnel rats found piles of smoldering torches, smashed and crumpled lanterns, and flaming barrels of oil. The smoke and shortage of oil to light the underground kingdom forced the tunnel rats to move into a few large rooms far from the oil stores. Packed too closely together and with too few comforts, tempers frayed. In the beginning, the rats argued, voices echoing down the tunnels. Soon, fists replaced words. Then blades replaced fists.

King Rat's control slipped with each raid we made.

Hiding well away in unused tunnels, our little band of rescued slaves had all the light they needed and more food than they could eat. Martin and I also had free run through more and more of the tunnels making up King Rat's underground empire. Given our wandering, it was only a matter of time before we found an exit out of the tunnels and up to the surface. When we did find it, we released all of the former slaves. Even better, it finally gave us a chance to get rid of Raoul.

True to his nature, Raoul doubted our intentions. "Are you releasing or taking me away for slaughter?"

"Oh dear, Martin, I believe Raoul has been down here so long he's become delirious."

"How can you tell, David?"

"Isn't it obvious? The poor prince has confused us with his mother's minions in the Tartegian court."

Raoul sputtered, too angry to form words.

"See, Martin? The poor Spare Prince has even lost the capacity for human speech."

"It is sad, David. We should release him into the wild so he can live out his few remaining days frolicking in the meadows."

"What a fine and humane idea, Martin! Let's do that."

After Raoul ascended the ladder and exited the tunnels—at sword point—we closed and locked the grating behind him.. Neither Martin nor I thought Raoul could lay his hands on any armed men, nor was he likely to be able to find his way through the tunnels beneath Beloren, but we saw no reason to take chances.

Free of helpless people to watch over, Martin and I made our way back to King Rat's shrunken domain.

As we neared the inhabited parts of the tunnel system, we heard many voices echoing down the tunnels. They seemed to all be repeating the same message, but with all the overlapping echoes, I couldn't make out what they were saying. It took ten minutes to get close enough to concentrate on a single voice.

"David Rice, His Majesty King Rat orders you to surrender! If you refuse, all of the remaining slaves in the kingdom will be fed to His Majesty's new tammar!"

# Chapter 27

*David*

The heralds' shouts echoed throughout the tunnels as Martin and I withdrew to discuss our options. With a sigh, Martin threw himself onto the tunnel floor

"This is why it's so hard to be the good guy. You try to do what's right and the next thing you know, the bad guy threatens innocent people unless you surrender. I spent years raiding north and south of the desert and you know what? No one ever threatened innocent bystanders in the hope of forcing me to surrender."

"Spend a little more time as a noble hero and you'll get used to it. At least it tells us that we're hurting King Rat. This place would fall apart without the slaves to do the work."

"Yeah, the same thought crossed my mind. Considering that, do you think the old rat boy will carry through with his threat, David?"

"After this very loud, very public announcement, I can't see how he has any other choice. I only see three possible outcomes. We defeat King Rat. King Rat captures us and feeds us to the tammar. Or a miracle occurs."

"I notice you left out King Rat feeding the slaves to the tammar."

"That's because I'll surrender to him before I let that happen."

"It won't come to that, David. I promised Callan I'd help get you back and I am *not* facing your wife again unless you are standing safely at my side! So, what do we do now?"

"We gather more information on King Rat's situation. With what little we know right now, I don't see how we can make any real plans. Are you up for some more exploration of his kingdom?"

"Sure. Are we looking for anything in particular?"

"The last time I paid a visit to King Rat's tammar pit, things didn't go so well for him *or* his tunnel rats. Whatever else the man is, he's not stupid. There's no way he'll ever rely on a rope tether to restrain his tammar again. He has to have changed the setup in the pit. We must discover what he has changed."

"It could take hours to find the pit on our own, especially if we have to dodge a lot of tunnel rats." Martin eyes lit up and he grinned. "So why don't we get a native to guide us to it!"

King Rat's heralds were positioned at the edges of his meager lighted territory, insuring their shouts reached our ears. Ever the thoughtful leader, he'd even sent a couple of guards to keep watch over each of his heralds. The heralds had been shouting their message so long that they and their guards had grown bored with the whole thing. They cried the message every few minutes, spending the rest of the time sitting around waiting.

"Hey, Jon, it's time to shout the message again."

"Let me skip this one, guys. My throat is raw." The herald's voice was getting raspy. "I've gotta rest it."

"Then this is your lucky day, Jon." I strode into the wavering circle of light cast by their torch. "I'm David Rice and I'm here to surrender."

All three men jumped to their feet in surprise. The guards raised their swords as the herald retreated behind them. My sword was sheathed at my side and I held my arms out wide, well away from the weapon.

They neither saw nor heard Martin dash up from behind them. He shoved the herald into the two guards. As the guards struggled for balance, Martin's sword pommel cracked against a guard's head. The first guard sagged to the floor, and Martin spun and delivered a similar blow to the second guard. The herald opened his mouth to cry for help. The cry froze in his throat as both of our swords pressed against his neck.

"Take your own advice and give your voice a rest," Martin said. "Unless David asks you a question, that is. Then you respond quickly and quietly. Do you understand?"

All too aware of the blades pricking his neck, the herald nodded his head very slowly.

"All right, David, you're up."

"King Rat says he wants to feed me to his tammar. I'll make it easy on him. Take me to King Rat's new tammar pit."

"I can't." The herald squeaked as Martin's sword drew a drop of blood. "I'm telling the truth! Nobody knows where it is except the king!"

# Chapter 28

*David*

"Why would that be a secret?"

"Ask King Rat if you really want to know," the herald muttered.

"Mind your manners, herald!" Martin punctuated his command by scratching the man's neck with his sword.

"I really don't know why it's a secret!" The herald pointed to one of the unconscious guards. "He says the king has been...twitchy...since you released that tammar. Some people think the tammar almost got King Rat and he's terrified of another one getting loose."

"But you're just guessing."

The herald nodded at my statement.

"It doesn't matter why he's keeping it secret, just that he is." I shook my head. "A better question is how he's keeping a place the size of a tammar pit secret?"

"There are a lot of tunnels down here. No one knows them all. Each day, the pit workers are blindfolded and the king personally leads them to the site," the herald replied. "He's threatened to execute anyone who tries to follow. Only the king and few of his guards know where the pit is."

"That's brutal, but I bet it's effective," Martin said.

"How long before the king leads another work party to the pit?"

"How should I know?" The herald sounded truly offended. "I am a herald of the court, not one of the lower classes!"

"That means you're pretty useless to us, aren't you?" Martin smacked the herald with his sword's pommel. "What do you want to do now, David?"

"I don't quite know," I responded. "I do find the whole idea behind a hidden tammar pit really odd. If King Rat wants to draw us into the open, why not announce a time and place for the big event?

He's got to know I'd try to stop him from feeding his slaves to the tammar!"

"Maybe King Rat is trying to confront us without the rest of the tunnel rats knowing about it? If he fails to capture us, only a few people would know his trap failed," Martin mused. "I don't know. That kind of plan is way too convoluted for my tastes. Of course, even you must admit you are known to take a very direct approach to problem solving. Maybe King Rat is counting on the shroud of secrecy to draw you into his trap?"

"If he's counting on that, let's give him exactly what he wants."

"I knew you were going to say that."

"Yes, you're very smart, Martin. So, if you were King Rat, where would you build the new tammar pit?"

"I would put it right where the old one was," Martin replied. "I'd make some changes—install a cage to keep the tammar from getting loose again—but otherwise, I wouldn't change much from the way it was before."

"I bow to your intimate knowledge of criminal affairs." I inclined slightly in Martin's direction. "Let's check it out."

"What about these guys?" Martin waved toward the unconscious guards and herald.

"Leave them. I don't want to stop and search for rope. Besides, as far as the herald knows, we believed his story and that's what he'll report to King Rat. That's assuming they even report this at all."

An hour later, we peeked down a dimly lit hallway toward the entrance to the old tammar pit. Six men guarded the doors. Martin had been right!

# Chapter 29

*David*

"David Rice, you've just found the tammar pit!" Despite the whisper, Martin still managed to sound like some kind of advertising huckster. "What are you going to do now?"

"Feeding you to the tammar has a certain appeal, right about now."

"Tsk, tsk, my boy. Is that any way to whisper to your best friend in the whole galaxy?"

"I'm going to go with 'yes' to that question."

"Perhaps this attitude explains why you had to crash land on a lost human colony to find a wife and a best friend. I recall advising you to work on your people skills when we were back in Faroon. It grieves me that you chose to ignore it."

"Then perhaps it's best if I stop inflicting my presence on you, dear friend. You asked what I'm going to do now? *I* will wait for those guards to escort the blindfolded workmen home from the construction site, slip inside, and find a hiding place within. Meanwhile, *you* are going to slip out of the tunnels and report to Callan."

"Oh, that is *so* not going to happen, David. I would face King Rat, all his guards, and a tammar, while I was armed with nothing more than a soup spoon, rather than face Callan and tell her I left you alone down here."

"Coward."

"When it comes to your wife, damn right I'm a coward! If I bring you back in one piece, I might get a peck on the cheek as thanks. *Might*. But if I leave you down here to die alone in these tunnels—even free and armed, as you are now—searchers will never even find my body! When my name is spoken within the palace, it will be in hushed whispers, serving solely to remind others the peril of interfering with your wife's love life!"

"Don't be melodramatic. Callan would never do that!"

Martin heaved a dramatic sigh. "No, she wouldn't harm a hair on my head. Instead, her eyes would fill with unshed tears, she would put on a brave face, then she would tell me your death wasn't my fault. What's worse is that she would mean every word of it." Martin shuddered. "I'd rather be flayed alive than face that!"

"Okay, okay. You can stay with me."

Martin grinned. "I knew you'd see the sense in my position, lad!"

We hung around watching the doors to the tammar pit for hours before anything happened. At least no one else wandered the halls, this being King Rat's big secret location and all. Finally, blindfolded workmen came out of the pit.

Watching the guards form around the workmen, I said, "What I don't understand is why use the blindfolds at all? The first time the workmen see the location, they're bound to recognize it."

"I can think of two reasons. First, it serves as a reminder to the workmen to keep their mouths shut about this place. Second, if anyone sees the guards escorting the workmen, the blindfolds reinforce the secrecy surrounding the project. But don't ask me why King Rat is bothering with all this hoopla, unless he's just paranoid. You do seem to have that kind of effect on certain people." Martin shook his head as if disappointed in me, somehow. "It all comes back to people skills, David."

Martin and I faded into the shadows of a side passage and watched the guards and workmen walk right past us. We waited five minutes before slipping down the tunnel and into the tammar pit. Burning torches filled sconces around the walls, making it easy for us to see how busy the workmen had been.

A steel cage stood in the center of the pit. A long, caged passage led from the main cage over to the far wall. The caged passage ended at a large door, surely used to let the tammar into and out of the cage. A double–gated cage entrance—similar in idea to the airlock in a spaceship—allowed guards to put victims into the cage without letting the tammar get its claws on the guards. Always the considerate ruler, King Rat had even ordered bleachers built around the cage. What was next, souvenirs and popcorn?

Distant voices interrupted our inspection of the new construction. The voices came from outside the pit, but they were growing louder by the second.

"King Rat must be in a hurry to complete this place. It sounds like he's ordered a second shift of workmen," Martin observed

"We'd better hide!"

"Good idea, David. Where?"

I looked about the pit. There was no place to hide!

# Chapter 30

*Callan*

When I had a chance to talk to the translator, I discovered he was the son for whom the tribal elder sought to purchase a wife. Tristan took great relish in relating the tale of the haggling over my bride price to the two of us. I smiled at the translator to show I was not offended.

Despite my smile, the man immediately prostrated himself before me, his arms outstretched and his nose touching the *Pauline's* deck. "I humbly beg pardon for my father's foolish and insulting attempt to buy you, Lady Death!"

"No apology is necessary. Fathers excel at embarrassing their children. Rise and think no more about it," I said. "And please call me Princess Callan or Your Highness—not Lady Death."

The man rose to his feet. "As you command, Lady Death."

His face turned red and he threw himself to the deck again. "I humbly beg your pardon, Lady– um, Princess Callan!"

"It was a mere slip of the tongue. Think nothing of it. Rise." I began to see why this man was still single. "What is your name?"

"Treb, Your Highness Princess Callan." He bowed deeply from the waist. At least he didn't drop to the deck again.

As the *Pauline* rose into the air, the squadron commander brought his ship alongside.

"Have you concluded your business with this desert tribe, Your Highness?"

"I have, Captain Dorrin. Is there something you wish from me?"

"Most definitely. I *wish* Her Highness would finally see fit to share the particulars of her plan with her squadron commander. I *wish* those particulars would include any further destinations you have in mind. It's so much easier to give proper orders to the airmen when one knows where one is going."

Lovely. My mother had chosen a prickly rules stickler to command my escort squadron. No doubt, mother hoped he would keep me from doing something she would call 'unwise.' A pedantic captain selected to counterbalance my impulsive nature—yes, it had Mother's fingerprints all over it.

"Of course, Captain! Nothing would please me more." I gave him my most dazzling smile. The airship's junior officers and airmen perked up and smiled in return. The captain continued gazing stolidly at me. "I would have gladly told you earlier, had you asked!"

"And I would gladly have asked earlier, had my airship been fast enough to catch up with your little ship." The good captain ground his teeth beneath his grimace of a smile. "But I am asking now, Your Highness."

"I am going to send an armed force into the tunnels of Beloren with the express intent of retrieving my husband and forcibly removing King Rat from his throne. The–"

A real smile broke across Captain Dorrin's face. "At last, someone is talking sense! My men are chomping at the bit to teach these tunnel rats a lesson, Princess Callan."

Behind Captain Dorrin, his men nodded enthusiastically.

"Why did you have us come all the way out here, Your Highness? Does this tribe know of hidden entrances to the tunnels?"

"I am afraid you have misinterpreted my intentions, Captain." My words summoned Dorrin's grimace back to prominence. "The force I will take into the tunnels must be one which cannot be traced to Mordan. David chose to surrender himself to King Rat to *avoid* drawing Mordan into a war with the city–states. I will not disregard the goal behind his sacrifice in order to rescue him."

"You wish to send a force of these desert tribesmen in place of my marines." Dorrin's tone was cold and formal in the extreme. "I see, Your Highness."

"Captain, were the consequences less dire, nothing would please me more than to have your marines storm the tunnels, slay the rats, and rescue David. I can think of no men I'd rather trust with David's life."

Dorrin's men straightened at the compliment, though their Captain appeared unconvinced.

"And yet you will send desert tribesmen instead."

"I did not negotiate for a raiding party, Captain. No tribesmen will attack the tunnels in place of your marines."

"Then who do you plan to send into the tunnels, Princess?"

"Correct me if I'm wrong, Captain, but I believe a battle is half won if the mere sight of your soldiers strikes fear into the hearts of your enemies."

"Of course, Your Highness. And there are no men on Aashla who inspire more fear than Mordanian marines."

"You are quite right, Captain. But I'm not going to send *men* into those tunnels."

The good captain blew out his breath in exasperation. "Please pardon an old navy man's ignorance, Your Highness, but who else *could* you send into the tunnels?"

"Trogs."

"Trogs? Absolutely not, Your Highness! I forbid it."

# Chapter 31

*Callan*

I gave Captain Dorrin the benefit of my most effective glare. It has everything; an arched eyebrow, folded arms, canted hips, a tapping foot, and smoldering eyes. Rob called it my Princess Glare and respected the effect it had on men. *Other* men, that is, as Rob was the one man completely unaffected by my glare.

The airmen crowding the rail shrank back from their captain, as if they expected him to burst into flames under the weight of the Princess Glare. I held my silence and waited for the captain to capitulate before my wrath. Captain Dorrin stood his ground, hands clasped behind his back, meeting the Princess Glare with a calm expression.

After nearly a minute, I admitted to myself that my glare was not working. What a horrible time to discover another man unaffected by it! Taking pity on Dorrin's men, I dropped the glare.

"You *forbid* me from pursuing my plan, Captain?" My tone implied my extreme disapproval of the captain's temerity.

"Even should it cost me my commission, I most assuredly do, Your Highness."

"My airship is faster than yours. We could simply outrun your squadron, Captain."

"Yes, but you could not pull away before I could order my men to attempt a boarding," Captain Dorrin responded. "Considering the risks of such a maneuver, I am confident you will not force me to endanger the lives of my men."

He was right, damn him. I relaxed my stance, nodding my head. "You are quite correct, Captain. Would you, at the very least, come aboard and allow me to explain my reasoning to you?"

"It will not sway my decision, Your Highness."

My arsenal of expressions was not limited to the Princess Glare. I reached into the arsenal and drew forth my Please Daddy look. That look had even worked on Rob—unless Mother was present. How fortunate she was far, far away.

"Please?"

My rising voice, subtly clasped hands, slightly canted head, and heavy-lidded eyes worked their magic. A paternalistic smile spread across the captain's face.

"Of course, Your Highness. Never let it be said I'm not a fair man."

As Nist brought the *Pauline* alongside Captain Dorrin's ship, Tristan murmured, "What is your plan, Princess?"

"Have you examined the good captain's left hand, Tristan?"

He did so. "All I see is a hand."

"Exactly!" Tristan still looked bewildered, so I added, "He wears no wedding band, nor is there any indication he has ever worn one. That means Captain Dorrin has no wife and, vastly more important, no daughters. I believe it is time to show the man just what he's been missing."

Tristan shuddered, backing away. "Try not to destroy the man, Princess."

Captain Dorrin hopped over the *Pauline's* rail. His body language screamed indulgence, making it that much easier for me to follow through with my plan.

I bowed my head but, through upraised eyes, met Captain Dorrin's gaze. Then I released all of the emotions I'd held in check ever since the envoy's ship carried David away from me. My voice trembled. My lips quivered. My breath caught with little hiccup sounds. My shoulders shook. My breast heaved. Tears streamed from my eyes.

Ten minutes later, we steamed off in search of a trog settlement.

# Chapter 32

*David*

Martin and I had a minute, maybe two, to get out of sight before the work party and their guards entered the tammar pit. We cast about for someplace—anyplace—to hide. Work progressed in every corner of the pit—from the arena to the ascending rows of benches for spectators—but provided no place where we could conceal ourselves. Even the hole in the ceiling—the one through which a bound Callan had been shoved into the tammar pit—was sealed.

"I only see one place to go." Martin pointed to the center of the pit.

The steel cage stretched from the floor to the ceiling, with both doors to the cage standing ajar. A cage–tunnel, for want of a better word for it, stretched from the large cage to a door in the back wall of the pit. No great leaps of imagination were required to figure out the tammar would enter and leave the pit through the cage–tunnel. Neither of us wanted to open that door, but we saw no other options.

Martin and I jumped into the pit, ran through the two gates, then headed down the cage–tunnel toward the door.

"Do you think we'll find a tammar on the other side of the door?" I asked.

"I'd bet on it. Too many things have been going our way lately for there not to be."

"We're trying to hide in a tammar lair while plotting to kill King Rat so he won't force the city–states to invade Mordan, and *that's* your idea of things going our way?"

"We've had free run of the tunnels for several days and are seriously irritating King Rat. And we're not dead yet," Martin shot back.

"When I relate this tale to my yet–to–be–conceived children, I do hope they find humor in your optimistic summation of our situation," I replied. "Lord only knows, I do not."

"That's hurtful, David. I'd even go as far as to say your words cut me to the quick!"

"Better my words than a tammar's claws, Martin. Or the swords and spears of a couple of dozen of King Rat's guards and workmen."

With workmen's voices drawing closer to the tammar pit entrance, Martin opened the door and we slipped through and into the lair. There wasn't one tammar to be found beyond the door—there were four!

# Chapter 33

*David*

Martin and I froze as the torch light reflected from two pairs of large, alert eyes. The owners of the eyes regarded us with an unsettling intensity, heads up and ears pricked forward. Their bodies almost quivered with tension as the tammars sized us up. The other two tammars slept—a small blessing, since most predators wake in a flash, but a blessing none–the–less.

Tearing my eyes from the tammars' stare, I studied the lair. It was about forty feet across and maybe thirty feet wide, with a sloping ceiling that started just higher than our heads but was close to thirty feet high at the far wall. The only door in that wall was twenty feet off the floor and behind a barred catwalk. We definitely weren't getting out that way.

"Why am I so good at predicting bad news?" Martin whispered through unmoving lips. "Have you got any brilliant ideas?"

"Go back the way we came?"

"What about the workmen and the guards?" Martin sidled closer to the door we'd come through.

"Let's put a door between us and the tammars before we waste time worrying about a bunch of tunnel rats."

Never taking my eyes from the tammars, my hand found the door handle. Slowly, ever so slowly, I turned the handle.

One tammar rose to its feet, extended its forelegs and stretched. A casual observer might have believed the tammar hadn't a care in the world. As an active participant in this drama, I saw it never took its eyes off of us.

"*Now!*" We shoved the door open and ran through it.

The two alert tammars sprang at us, closing the gap with terrifying speed!

"*Boost!*" I cried to Martin while triggering my own Boost.

Time slowed as adrenaline flooded my body. The charging tammars seemed to slow, as well, but the huge predators still moved much faster than even a Boosted human could run. Martin and I threw our whole bodies into shutting the door, trying desperately to close it before the tammars reached it.

We were still a foot short of closing the door when the two beasts crashed into it. Our Boosted strength was nothing against the combined might of two tammars. Martin and I were thrown backward twenty feet as the door slammed open. The two tammars bounded into the pit, with the other two tammars close on their tails!

# Chapter 34

*David*

Flung from the door, Martin and I tucked and spun and landed on our feet. Had we landed on our backs—a certainty if we had not Boosted—the tammars would never have allowed us to regain our feet. As it was, we still had fifty feet of cage-tunnel to cover just to reach the full-sized cage. But if we could get to the cage, we had a fighting chance. The cage-tunnel was so narrow the tammars would be forced to come at us one at a time. With Boost, plus the freedom of movement afforded by the larger cage, maybe Martin and I could block the tammars from leaving the cage-tunnel. I had no idea what we would do after that, but decided to solve my problems one at a time.

The two lead tammars took a second to check their environment. I assume instinct drove them to look for threats, but anything that slowed them down was fine by me!

"Run!" Martin cried.

"No, swing!" I grabbed the bars above our heads, pulled my feet up, and began swinging along the bars of the cage-tunnel like some jungle lord from the adventure vids my father and I loved to watch.

Martin followed my lead just as the tammars decided it was safe to chase us. For most people, running *was* faster. With our Boost-enhanced strength and reflexes, Martin and I were much faster swinging.

The charging tammars snarled and snapped, getting in each other's way, each eager to be the first to make a kill. Despite their fighting, the closest tammar was only fifteen feet behind us as Martin and I swung into the full-sized cage. The first gate out of the cage hung open on the far side of the pit. It was no more than thirty feet away, but it might as well have been in Mordan for all the good it did. Martin and I knew the chase would be over for us if the tammars reached open space and could leap properly.

192

Beyond the cage, the pit echoed with the shouts of the workmen and the guards just entering the room. In seconds, the normal beginning–of–shift chatter gave way to cries of alarm.

"The tammars are free!"

"The gate is open!"

"It's Rice and Bane!"

"Let's get out of here!"

"Bar the doors!"

"Alert the king!"

"Ask for more reinforcements!"

The workmen were as scared of Martin and me as they were of the tammars! In other circumstances, I'd have enjoyed the notoriety we had earned among the tunnel rats. At the moment, I was happy they were running from us rather than firing crossbows at us.

At the end of the cage–tunnel, we drew our swords and prepared to fight the tammars!

# Chapter 35

*David*

The first tammar leapt while it was still in the cage–tunnel. The bars rang from the impact of skull on steel and the tammar's charge slowed. I took advantage of its disorientation and slashed it across the cheek. Skin parted, blood flowed, and the tammar roared in pain. It swatted at my blade and, despite my Boost–enhanced speed, was quick enough to smack the blade tip. The tammar yowled as the tip of my sword plunged into its paw. The creature yanked its paw back, but the power of its blow almost knocked the sword from my hand!

I stepped back from my thrust, leaving the way clear for Martin. With a shout, he lunged at the angry predator. The tammar reared up on its hind legs, whacking its head on the low bars a second time. A line of blood welled behind Martin's blade as he scored a cut on the tammar's leg. He leapt back just ahead of a slashing claw from the second tammar, which we had thought blocked from the fight. When the first tammar reared, the second one saw an opening between the first tammar's legs and swiped through the legs. Its trickery almost caught Martin.

The first tammar dropped back to all fours and discovered the second tammar between its legs. With a yowl of protest, it raked its back claws in the other one's face, driving the second predator back behind it again.

"Martin, these things are too big and too fast for us. There's no way we can keep them bottled up long enough to kill one of the tammars, much less all four!" I lunged for the tammar's right eye but ended up slicing through an ear.

"What do you suggest we do?" Martin tried for the other eye but his blade just scraped along the jawbone.

"One of us must attack from a safer direction. You run out of the cage and attack this beast through the bars of the cage–tunnel." I stabbed at a slashing paw and missed. The paw missed me, as well, but came within an inch of gutting me.

"Why me?" Martin asked.

"Because I've done a lot more Boosting than you have. I'm acclimated to it and can keep it going longer than you," I replied, slashing a leg. "Now go!"

Someone else—such as my wife, to select an example purely at random—would have argued with me. Martin and I both had Scout training and, more, both knew I was the logical man to guard the tunnel. Martin made a wild swing to force the tammar back then bolted for the cage door.

I moved to block the center of the tunnel exit and stood alone against the tammars!

# Chapter 36

*David*

The second tammar got tired of waiting for a chance to get at me. It slashed the right flank of the tammar I had been fighting. A roar turned into a yowl as the wounded tammar's rear leg collapsed under the force of the blow. The impatient tammar started climbing over the lead tammar, pulling itself over that tammar with its claws.

As its flanks were ripped up, the tammar before me screamed in pain and fury. By instinct, it reared up on its hind legs to throw the enemy off of its back. As before, it banged its head on the bars over the cage–tunnel. As an added bonus, it whacked the second tammar's head against the bars, as well. Stunned, both tammars reeled as if drunk.

Seizing the opening their power struggle provided, I lunged at the wounded and distracted predator. My blade struck true, piercing the tammar's left eye and plunging into its brain! In a move my hoped–for children would probably find morbidly fascinating, I rotated my sword left to right, up and down, then back again. The blade cut up the tammar's eye but, more importantly, it also sliced the tammar's brain into many parts.

The tammar pulled away from me in reflex, almost jerking my sword from my hand. I'd been expecting that reaction, though. Using a two–handed grip, I held onto my sword and pulled it free. The tammar spasmed and convulsed in violent death throes as the last impulses from its destroyed brain went awry. The impatient tammar found itself flung left and right, unable to get past the dying predator.

That's when Martin dashed up to the side of the cage–tunnel. He thrust his sword into the throat of the impatient tammar and sawed through muscle and arteries. Blood fountained from the tammar, soaking it and its dying companion.

"The tunnel is blocked, David!" Martin shouted over the screams of the dying and trapped tammars. "Get out of there before the other two start clawing their way over the two dead ones!"

I sprinted for the cage door. Behind me, the two healthy tammars were already clawing at the dying ones, trying to get past them so they could get their paws on me. I reached the door before either of them could pull their way past the two corpses and out into the full-sized cage. With great satisfaction, I slammed the inner cage door shut. With a clang, the door rebounded and swung open again.

The first tammar was poking its head out of the cage–tunnel when I saw that the inner door had no latch. It took but a glance to see the same was true of the outer door. I had no way to lock the tammars into the cage!

# Chapter 37

*David*

"There's no latch!" I yelled.

"Lovely. I guess it's on backorder with the locksmith," Martin replied.

We both looked about for something to use to block one of the gates or fasten a gate to the cage bars. There were no spools of wire, no stacks of steel bars, and no handy padlock large enough to fit around the bars. Nor were there any wooden crates, large or small, we could push in front of the outer cage gate to slow down the tammar and buy us a few seconds to scramble for the door out of the pit. We would have to deal with the guards and the workmen, but right then two dozen men were much less intimidating than two tammars.

A boom echoed through the pit. The workmen and guards had slammed shut the only door out of the pit. A crash followed the boom; the guards barring the door, I guessed. Our only hope for escape was blocked. We no longer had any other choices open to us. Martin and I either found a way to deal with the tammars or the tammars would deal with us with gnashing teeth and slashing claws!

I glanced back at the cage–tunnel. One of the two remaining tammars clawed and wriggled its way past the two tammars Martin and I had already slain. We had mere seconds before that tammar came bounding across the pit floor and out of the cage. Even Boosted, there was no way I could get back inside the cage and slay the creature before it was free. Martin could kill it through the bars, except the tammar was on the other side of the cage–tunnel, far beyond Martin's reach.

Martin saw that, too. He crouched, then sprang up to the top of the cage–tunnel. Even Boosted, clearing the thing in a single bound was beyond his strength. Instead, Martin turned the leap into a vault. Grabbing a bar over the top, he swung his feet around toward the far side of the tunnel. It was a great move, just the kind of thing you'd see from the swashbuckling hero in an adventure vid. But, with his concentration on the nearly-free tammar, Martin's hand planted too near the fourth tammar.

I saw a tawny blur as the tammar's claw lashed at Martin's hand. Blood spurted over the bars. His hand ripped open, Martin lost his grip on the bar. With a cry of agony, Martin collapsed onto the bars at the top of the cage-tunnel. He lay within easy reach of the tammar below.

Another claw slashed at Martin and there was nothing I could do to help him!

# Chapter 38

*David*

I charged around the cage toward Martin, hoping for a miracle. Maybe the tammar would strike a bar instead of flesh. Or maybe something even less probable would happen and save my friend.

Then Martin rolled over on the bars, bringing his unwounded sword arm down against the bars. Was he crazy, trapping his sword at his side like that? Then Martin shoved his upper body up and away from the bars with his sword arm. At the last second, he also snatched his good hand away from the bars. Martin's timing was perfect. The tammar's claw slashed beneath him, tearing his shirt sleeve but missing the hand and arm!

Dropping back toward the bars, Martin swung his sword between the bars of the cage–tunnel and slashed the tammar's eyes. With a yowl, the tammar rolled away, its paws batting at the sword, which Martin had already pulled back out of its reach.

Cradling his wounded hand, Martin jumped down next to the tammar attempting to pull itself past the two dead tammars. Martin stumbled on the landing, another cry of pain escaping his lips as he steadied himself with his wounded hand. Rising, he drove his sword again and again into the body of the tammar squirming to get past its dead companions. By the time I reached his side, the cage–tunnel was completely blocked by three dead tammars. The fourth, its eyes cut, slunk back toward the tammar lair at the end of the cage–tunnel.

"Sit down before you fall down," I said, catching his left arm at the elbow and helping him down.

"Does my hand look as bad as it feels?" Martin put on a brave smile to mask the pain. "I do hope not, because it feels terrible."

"There's too much blood for me to say. I'll let you know when I can stop the bleeding and get a good look. This is going to hurt, Martin."

I tore my shirt off and pressed it hard against the shredded palm. Martin hissed but held his hand steady.

"What a pity Callan isn't here to see you," Martin said through gritted teeth. "Here's her heroic husband, shirtless, stained with the blood of men and beasts, and glistening with sweat. I do believe we'd have a little heir in the making in no time!"

"I had no idea my love life was of such interest to you, Martin."

"It's not, but I'll try anything to keep my mind off of my hand right now."

I worked fast, following my Scout training and drawing on the information fed to me from my implant. In the wider galaxy, medical nanites would repair the worst of the damage to Martin's hand in an hour or two. Here on Aashla...

The damage to the hand was extensive and blood kept oozing, making it difficult to get a clear look at the wound. Eventually, my implant built a clear image of the hand from the brief glimpses I got after wiping away blood. Three slashing cuts had opened the hand to the bones. None of those bones were broken, but I couldn't tell if tendons or ligaments were damaged. On top of all that, dirt from the tammar's claw and from the pit floor had worked into the wound. All in all, the hand was a medical mess.

"I'm no doctor, so take what I say with a grain or two of salt. But it's possible you're going to lose that hand, Martin."

# Chapter 39

*David*

With the bleeding slowed down to a slow ooze, there was little more I could do for Martin's hand. Using strips torn from my shirt, I bound the wounded hand against his chest.

"This ought to help with the bleeding, Martin. According to my implant, immobilizing the hand should help with the pain, too."

Martin watched me work without really focusing on what I was doing. "So, I might lose the hand, huh?"

"Yeah. Maybe. I'm not a doctor, Martin. I mean, who knows what Tristan can do when he gets a chance to work on it? He saved me when I took that crossbow bolt through the chest. He might be able to save your hand, too."

Martin nodded absently. "Right... You know, if I do lose the hand, I'll be unconscious by the time the doctor finishes cutting it off. So, you have to promise to do something for me, David."

"You want me to give the hand a proper burial? Maybe have a carpenter construct a miniature coffin and hire a priest to say a few words over it?"

"Hm? Those are all good ideas, but they're not what I had in mind. Promise me you'll have the doctor give me a nice, shiny hook to replace the hand."

"A hook? Why would you want that? Have you got some strange desire to frighten little children or something?"

"You disappoint me, David. I thought you watched lots of old adventure vids when you were a kid. Raider? Pirate? Hook? How much more traditional can you get?"

"A hook. Right. Tell you what, Martin, let's worry about that *after* we get out of these tunnels with our lives."

"That's an excellent point, lad! And have you concocted any brilliant plans for doing that?"

"I've got an idea, though its brilliance is questionable. Last time I was down here, there was a big opening in the ceiling right above us. King Rat's pit master dropped victims through it to the tammar waiting below." I tied off the last of the bindings holding Martin's arm against his chest. "It's been sealed off, but I'll bet they left it till the end of the rebuilding. It would have been too useful for dropping construction supplies to the pit floor. If I'm lucky, they've only completed the first layer of plaster, meaning it will be fairly thin. Sit back and try to relax for a few minutes. I'm going to try to knock an escape hole in King Rat's new ceiling!"

I scrabbled through the tools left by the workmen, selecting a hefty hammer I could swing with one arm. Climbing one of the cage bars, I leaned out from the bar as far as possible and started whacking the new plaster. The angle was awkward and my shoulder and arm ached within minutes, but I made fast progress. Then, over the sounds of breaking plaster, we heard shouted orders outside the door.

Reinforcements for King Rat's guard squad had arrived!

# Chapter 40

*Callan*

I rubbed my arms, feeling the goosebumps. The night air was cold five thousand feet above the ground. Below us, the moonlight did little to illuminate Beloren. I couldn't imagine how Nist saw well enough to spot the navel squadron, much less know when it was in position.

My heart hammered in my chest and my mind played over the events of the last few days. Convincing Captain Dorrin to follow my lead had been child's play compared to what had come afterwards.

Finding a trog tribe, which I'd expected to be difficult, was easy. Treb, the translator, led us directly to a tribe no more than an hour's flight from his own desert camp. Despite working through a translator using sign language, negotiations sped along nicely once the trogs discovered Lady Death was present. The ceremony in my honor, though, took hours. Worse, the next three trog tribes we visited also insisted on bestowing similar honors on me.

The trogs' veneration yielded one benefit—it impressed the heck out of Captain Dorrin and his men. The good captain offered no further arguments against my plan. That was a relief, as I doubted histrionics would work on him a second time.

When we finally found the Great One, he readily agreed to my plan. For centuries, the city-states waged a war of extermination against the trogs. He leapt at the chance to strike a blow against the largest and wealthiest among those city-states.

Then the true planning began. My plan had been simple—take a bunch of trogs into the tunnels, wipe out the tunnel rats and their odious king, then rescue David. Its simplicity horrified Captain Dorrin and his marine commander. After hearing the gist of the marine commander's plan, the Great One was convinced to turn away from my smash-and-grab approach, as well.

I readily admit the marine commander's plan was better than mine, but it was more complex. It required supplies and large-scale transportation and coordinated action. I came to hate the word 'logistics' long before the military leaders were satisfied with their plan.

David had been underground for days and days before we were ready to strike. At long last, though, it was almost time to act.

"What you see?" The Great One wouldn't come within five feet of the *Pauline's* railing. Who'd have thought the mighty leader of the trogs feared heights?

"I see a huge light spot where Beloren should be," I said. "And I see a big dark spot where everything else should be. Maybe Nist can tell us what he sees?"

"Of course, Lady Death!"

Nist loved my new nickname and used it every chance he got. It did demonstrate a certain level of familiarity I'd wanted, so I strove for regal forbearance. I arched an eyebrow and waited for Nist to continue.

"The squadron is approaching the city from the north, as planned. The Beloren patrol ships haven't spotted them yet, but they will within the minute."

I leaned over the rail a bit, trying to see what Nist saw. Behind me, a soft moan slipped through the Great One's lips. It was a good thing the rest of his band of warriors were below deck, unable to see and hear his fear!

I pointed toward a darker than normal blob outside Beloren. "Is that the naval squadron?"

"Uh, no Lady Death. That's a herd of cattle. The squadron is over there."

I followed Nist's pointing finger. It was just more darkness to me.

"I'll take your word for it, Nist."

"Ah ha! The squadron has been spotted and the Beloren patrol ships are moving to intercept!" Nist said. "Hang on, Lady Death. Our descent will be rapid."

I turned to the Great One. "You may want to go below to...prepare your warriors."

The Great One nodded and scrambled below.

Then the *Pauline* angled down and dove for the heart of Beloren!

# Chapter 41

*Callan*

Milo sauntered to the bow of the *Pauline*. He was as comfortable on the sloping deck of the airship as he'd been in the palace and in the streets of Faroon. I meet people from all walks of life and with wide ranging abilities, but I've never met anyone quite like Milo. He truly is an amazing young man who impresses me more and more with each passing day. With the right training and education, I believe there is nothing Milo cannot do.

"What's bothering His Greatness? Looking at him, I finally understand what people mean when they say someone is green around the gills."

"As best I can tell, the smartest, mightiest, greatest trog warrior of all time is deathly afraid of heights."

"We've got a solid deck beneath us." The ship angled down some more and Milo grabbed a nearby stay. "Well, it's *mostly* beneath us! What is he scared of?"

I'd grown up around and on airships and always felt at home on board them. But I also remembered falling from Martin's airship at the trading post in the desert. Without David and a lot of luck, I'd have died that day.

"Have you ever been hurt in a long fall, Milo?"

"Nope. I'm too quick to have falls like that."

"How about falling dreams? I'm told everyone has those."

"Yeah, I've had those. They can be scary, but they're just dreams. They can't hurt you."

"No, they can't. But those dreams are so strong for some people that their minds recall them even when they are awake."

"So, it's like the Great One looks over the railing and can't help seeing himself falling?"

The memory of plunging from the airship returned, unbidden, and I shuddered. "That's the way it's been with me since..."

Milo linked his arm through mine. "I won't let you fall, Callan."

I wrapped my hand around his arm, holding on more tightly than I'd intended. "Thank you, Milo."

Rousing myself from my months–old memory, I changed the subject. "Can you see in this darkness? You're the one who has to guide Nist to the drop–off point."

"Oh, yeah– I mean, yes Your Highness! I found that sewer entrance David took when he rescued you from the tunnel rats and then scouted out the alley it's in. It was easy to find the building you guys ran to after getting away last time you were here."

"Are you sure you can find that building from the air and in the dark?"

"I've already found the building. It's right over there, Your Highness."

As usual, I saw nothing but varying depths of darkness.

"You called me Callan just a few seconds ago. Why have you suddenly gone all formal on me?"

Milo fidgeted for a second before answering. "I was giving comfort to you, then. And that's got to be personal, right?"

I leaned down and kissed Milo on the cheek. God, this boy was going to break a lot of hearts growing up. But the girl who captured *his* heart would be lucky, indeed!

"Yes, Milo, you're absolutely right. And thank you for the personal touch. But that doesn't explain your formal address."

"We're on the mission now. I'm using your title to show respect for you and your authority."

"Which guard told you that?"

"Captain Hunter. He's been training me some in his spare time."

It seems David and I weren't the only ones who recognized Milo's potential. I made a mental note to thank Captain Hunter when we got home.

"I've got to guide Nist the rest of the way into the city. Will you be okay up here alone, Your Highness?"

"I will now, Milo. Go on back to Nist."

Milo slipped off into the darkness. Murmured conversation rose from the pilot's controls and, a couple of minutes later, Nist leveled off the *Pauline*. Seconds later, he settled over a building. As the airship slowed, the Great One and two dozen of his best warriors came on deck.

"We aren't far from the entrance to the tunnels. With the exception of David—the Hand of Death, if you prefer—and Martin Bane, anyone you see down there is an enemy. If they run away, let them go. If they try to stop us, kill them."

I swung my legs over the railing. "Now let's go get my husband back!"

# Interlude

*David is Twenty-one*

"David Eliot Rice, with highest honors."

The faculty applauded politely, my family with more vigor. Dad's piercing whistle rose over it all.

The light applause died down as I walked across the stage to accept my commission from the academy commander. And that's when my sister added her two credits to the proceeding.

"Woo hoo! Now he's off to find his spacebabe!"

I gave Sandra props for impeccable timing. Her voice carried to every corner of the amphitheater. Laughter rippled through the crowd, even though few of them understood the comment. My handful of friends in the academy roared, though. I'm sure Sandra swelled in pride at their laughter.

"Congratulations, Scout Second Class Rice." The commander shook my hand as he presented my commission.

"Thank you, Commander Gordon."

"I thought I had heard it all, Rice, but 'spacebabe' is a new one on me."

"It's a private joke, sir."

"And the young lady?"

"My little sister, sir."

"You may not believe it now, but you'll miss her once you're Out There."

"I am certain I will, sir, but please don't tell *her* that."

Commander Gordon laughed and released my hand. Back straight and eyes front, I left the stage.

Twenty minutes later, my family wrapped me in a big hug. Yes, even my little sister joined in.

Mom wiped away tears. "I'm so proud of you, honey!"

"We all are," Dad added.

"Speak for yourself!" Sandra socked me in the arm. "Okay, yeah, I'm proud of you, too, big brother. Hey, did you hear me holler when that old guy gave you your commission?"

"Yes, O Annoying One, you yelled loud enough that I bet they heard you on Terra!"

"You think so?"

Sandra grinned so brightly I couldn't help but grin back.

Mom caught my arm. "I stopped by the nursing home to visit Mr. Hart a couple of days ago. He's just as proud of you as we are."

"Really? How's he doing?"

Mom bit her lip, telegraphing bad news. "Not well, son. The nurses think he's holding on until your graduation. Are you going to visit him before leaving for your training mission?"

"You know I am, Mom. I was planning to go tomorrow."

"As much as we want to celebrate with you, David, you should see him today. Tomorrow may be too late."

Three hours later, the head nurse at Mr. Hart's home smiled warmly as I entered her section.

"Hello, David. Don't you look handsome in your dress uniform!" She nodded her head down the hall. "He's waiting for you."

It had only been three months since I'd last been here to visit Mr. Hart, but his condition shocked me. He looked so frail, just skin and bones. But his eyes lit up when he saw me.

I snapped off my best academy salute. "Scout Second Class David Rice reporting, sir!"

He laughed and it turned into a cough.

"It's good to see you, David. Come over here and let me get a good look at you."

I sat on the edge of the bed and fought to keep a smile on my face and tears from my eyes. Mr. Hart took my hand in both of his, patting it absently.

"I'm glad I got a chance to see you before I go, David."

"I'm the one who's going, Mr. Hart. I leave on my training mission in two days. I can't wait to tell you all about it when I get back."

"You do that, lad. Your parents will know where to find me."

"Yeah, right here in this room!"

"Don't kid yourself, David. I've had a good run, but now I'm run down. It's about time to scout out what comes next."

I blinked back the tears which suddenly filled my eyes. "At least you'll be with Princess Audrey and good ol' Roy."

"There is that, lad. There is that."

Mr. Hart's eyes fluttered and closed. It wasn't until the head nurse came that I realized my old friend had slipped away.

She left me alone with him for a few more minutes. When she returned, she handed a small box to me.

"Mr. Hart wanted you to have this after he passed. Your visits meant a lot to him, David. I wish all my patients had people like you."

The box held Mr. Hart's rank insignia and a short note.

*David, I'd be honored if you wore my insignia during your service. Thank you for spending time with an old man and listening to my stories. Every man has a princess waiting for him somewhere. May you find yours out among the stars.*

I had to get the nurse to pin Mr. Hart's insignia on my uniform. I couldn't see through my tears. I stayed with him until the men from the morgue came to take his body away. I snapped to attention and held my salute until his body was out of sight. My heart heavy, I headed back to the academy.

Two days later, I began searching for my spacebabe.

# Chapter 42

*David*

The sounds of shouting and banging grew louder outside the door to the tammar pit. The banging faded away as the shouting both grew louder and developed a cadence. The door made it impossible to understand what the men were shouting, but it sounded as if they were psyching themselves up to charge into the room and attack. Did they expect to fight tammars as well as a couple of scouts? I hoped so. In our current state—with Martin wounded and me tiring from swinging the hammer—the tunnel rats would definitely capture us or kill us unless we climbed out of the pit.

I made steady progress smashing through the new ceiling with the hammer, but would steady progress be enough? Should I Boost so soon after the last time or should I save it for the fight yet to come? Just as I concluded Boost was called for, the hammer broke through the new ceiling! Plaster rained to the floor below.

"Hey, give a guy some warning!" Martin squawked, scurrying out from under the plaster drop zone.

The hole was far too small for us to fit through, but it wouldn't be for long. I smacked the ceiling from below, then hooked the hammer through the hole and pulled on the plaster from above. Alternating pounding and pulling created a network of cracks. Seconds later, a big chunk of ceiling crashed to the floor of the tammar pit.

Reaching through the hole, I grabbed the edge of the floor above and pulled myself up into the darkness.

"Bring the torch directly beneath the hole," I called.

Enough light shone through the hole to give dim illumination in the room above the pit. It was just as I remembered, including stout ropes dangling from half a dozen pulleys. Grabbing the closest rope, I tied a loop at the end of it and lowered it to Martin. Tossing the torch up to me, he secured one foot in the loop and held onto the rope with his good hand. With a nod from Martin, I hauled on the rope. It slithered through the pulleys and began reeling him up.

Martin hung midway between the pit floor and the ceiling when I heard the door to the tammar pit fly open.

King Rat commanded, "Crossbowmen! Shoot that man hanging on the rope!"

# Chapter 43

*David*

So much for using the pulley to gently and easily lift Martin! King Rat's command dictated speed and brute strength. I hauled on the rope for all I was worth, but it seemed as if Martin barely moved. Working hand over hand was too slow, but what other option did I have? Then the first crossbow twanged and a quarrel flashed just beneath Martin's feet.

"Faster would be better, David!"

Martin spoke too fast, his words sharp and clipped and seeming all the more urgent as a result. Martin must have Boosted, but I could not imagine what he hoped to gain.

Glancing through the hole, I watched Martin lean out from the rope as a quarrel flew through the space he'd just cleared. As quickly, he ducked under a second quarrel, which missed his head by inches! That answered my question. His Boost was buying me the extra couple of seconds I needed to pull Martin to safety!

Martin dodged two more quarrels and even kicked one aside with his free foot.

"Stop dodging or you won't be able to come through this hole!" I called.

Putting the rope over my shoulder, I ran directly away from the hole. The pulleys squeaked and whined as the rope spun through them.

I heard Martin taunt the crossbowmen one last time, then he flew up through the jagged hole I'd created and stepped onto the floor.

Below, King Rat roared, "Imbeciles! How could all of you miss a man dangling right in front of you! If Rice and Bane escape, I'll feed each of you to my tammars!"

King Rat must have been really focused on us not to have noticed the three dead tammars in the pit. Martin, considerate man that he is, took time to enlighten King Rat.

"Hey rat boy," Martin yelled, "take a look at the pit floor. You should stop using the plural form of tammar!"

Silence fell below us, then an inarticulate roar of rage echoed around the pit and through the hole.

"I'm afraid we broke three of your toys. But don't worry, you won't live long enough to miss them!" Martin called. Flashing a grin my way, he said, "It's the simple pleasures that make life worth living, David. Never forget that."

Then we heard massed footsteps coming from the tunnel outside our room. King Rat had sent guards through the tunnels to block our escape!

# Interlude

*Callan is Twenty*

Heat weighed down upon me, sapping my energy. Rob led eight men, all who remained of my full guard contingent, and me deeper into the desert. He set a fast pace, putting as much distance between us and our raider pursuers as possible. Sand swirled around us, working into our clothing and scratching and chafing our skin.

"There's cover ahead, men!" Rob's voice remained strong, calm, and clear, giving no indication of despair or fatigue.

I struggled to raise my head and look where Rob pointed. A jumble of rocks rose from the desert, the dark gray standing out in sharp contrast to the blinding white sand all around us.

I stumbled and would have sprawled into the sand had one of my guards not caught me. He wrapped an arm around my waist, keeping me on my feet.

"Lean on me, Your Highness."

"Th–thank you, Hoskins."

"It is my honor and my job, Your Highness."

Hoskins—Charlie to his friends—was close to my own age. A tall, strong man filled with good humor and dedication to his duty. In other circumstances, we could have been friends, perhaps more than friends. Instead, a vast gulf yawned between his station and mine. The gulf was not insurmountable, but a man like Charlie Hoskins could only bridge it with deeds of valor so great as to be beyond the abilities of most men.

Was it possible Hoskins could be the hero I'd searched for all these years? God only knew, we needed that hero right now. I could but hope that Hoskins, or one of my other guards, proved to be him.

With Hoskins' aid, I made it to the rocks. Hoskins and Rob saw me settled into shade cast by the rocks. Rob organized the camp with typical efficiency before returning to me.

"How are you, Little One?"

"Our situation must be truly desperate. You haven't called me Little One since I turned twelve."

A rueful smile spread across Rob's face. "As I recall, you nearly bit my head off for using a little girl's nickname."

I laughed without much humor. "I really was a brat, wasn't I?"

I expected Rob to offer a playful reply, make some attempt to cheer me up.

"No, Callan, you were never a brat. You have been difficult, willful, curious, and kind. But never a brat." Rob turned a serious face my way. "I hope you will forgive an old man's impertinence, but I am proud of the young woman you've become. You are a credit to your parents and your country."

"We aren't getting out of this one, are we, Rob?"

"And now I'm reminded that I left intelligent and observant off of my list of your qualities." Rob looked off into the distance. "We still live, Your Highness, and that is something."

"Call me Callan, Rob. Here at the end, I want no titles between us."

"I shall call you Callan only until such time as you are safe. And safe you may yet be. After all..."

Rob trailed off, leaving me to complete his oft-used saying.

"Where there is life, there is hope."

Rob turned his gaze back to me and this time his eyes held a true twinkle. "Besides, Callan, your hero could still arrive in time to save the day."

"Do you think he's just going to pop up out of the sand, Rob?"

"Or he could drop out of the sky. Honestly, I care not–"

*"Trogs! To arms! Trogs are upon us!"*

Blue–skinned terrors, creatures I'd seen only in illustrations, charged around the rocks not fifty yards from us and rushed toward our little camp. I counted ten and they still came. Then twenty. I stopped at thirty.

"Stay against the rocks, Callan. We will form a cordon and keep you safe for as long as possible. Take up a sword if you can and if you must."

Drawing his sword, Rob turned away.

"Rob?"

He looked over his shoulder.

"Thank you. For everything."

Rob sketched a salute and began organizing our defenses.

"I love you as I love my father."

Between the shouts and a strange, ear-shattering boom in the distance, he didn't hear me. He knew my feelings for him, but I wanted him to hear me say it.

Then the trogs were upon us and I could but watch as my guards, my brave defenders, fell one after the other before the trogs' superior numbers. Far too soon, only Rob and Hoskins still stood. I hefted a sword and waited to take my place in the fight. Seconds later, a spear plunged into Hoskins chest. With his dying breath, my youngest guard struck down the trog before him.

And so I took Hoskins place next to Rob, expecting nothing but a quick and painful death.

A loud, sharp crack sounded from above us and a small crater blew out in the ground beside the trogs. All eyes, trog and human alike, turned to see the cause. A man stood atop the rocks, some device clutched in one hand.

The man shouted in a language strange to me. The trogs shouted in return and most of them charged the man.

"This may be our chance to insure your survival, Callan. Be prepared to flee on my command."

Then the man on the rocks *moved*, and he was like nothing I had ever seen before. In a second he twisted, turned, dodged, and danced among the trogs. And where he went, death followed. He ripped through our enemies like a scythe through wheat.

Rob tore his gaze from the amazing spectacle, launching an attack against the closest trogs. Three minutes later, this amazing man rammed a spear through the last of the trogs and we were saved.

He met my eyes and a broad smile spread across what I now realized was a quite handsome face.

I smiled in return. "You have saved us. How can I thank you?"

He spoke in the strange language again and then collapsed.

Rob and I rushed to his side. We found no wounds and the man still lived.

"Considering how he moved and fought, I suspect the man is simply exhausted, Your Highness."

I barely heard Rob as I drank in the sight of the man.

"He came, Rob."

"Hm? I'm sorry, what did you say, Your Highness?"

"He came. When we least expected him and when we most needed him. I'd stopped believing in him. I'd stopped looking for him. And yet he still came, Rob. At long last, my hero is here."

# Chapter 44

*Callan*

I'd spent no more than a minute on this roof, but that minute was tied to the deepest of emotions. Fear, anger, and gut–wrenching loss rose unbidden when my feet touched the roof for a second time. Fear that those wretched tunnels would take another precious life from me. Anger at King Rat for all he had done to me, past and present. The gut–wrenching loss I still felt for Rob.

I stared off into the night, suppressing my emotions. When this night was over, I would give rein to them. But until David and I were free of this city, such emotions were distractions I could not afford.

Milo touched my shoulder. "We're ready, Your Highness."

"Thank you, Milo." I turned to face the Great One. "You know the plan. You know the stakes. Do you have any questions?"

"No."

"Then follow me."

I led the trogs down the stairs attached to the outside of the building, to the alley below. Once we were on the ground, Milo took the lead.

"You're sure this is the way?" I asked.

"Yes, Your Highness. After Martin showed me how to get into the tunnels, I memorized the alleys all around the entrance," he said. "If we have to run I won't lead us into any dead ends."

"That was clever thinking on your part. We'll make a guard out of you, yet."

"Nah, I'm going to be a spy. Captain Hunter says my um...skill set...is better suited for that sort of thing."

Did he, now? I edited my mental note of appreciation to Captain Hunter for training Milo. It's not that Hunter's assessment was wrong—Milo had the makings of an excellent spy—but I had bigger plans for my young friend. Those plans included a stability sorely lacking in his life thus far.

Moments later, Milo stopped at an opening in the ground. "This is it!"

"Good job, Milo." I turned to the Great One. "Send your warriors below. I'll be right behind you." I turned back to Milo. "You stay here and wait for us."

"Oh no you don't. I'm coming with you, Callan!"

"Absolutely not! I promised Kim I'd keep you safe. She would kill me if something happened to you."

"Death is nothing compared to what *I'd* face from David if something happened to *you*."

"You know David would never hurt you, Milo."

"I know he wouldn't hurt me. But he would be *disappointed* in me if you got hurt. He'd try to hide it, but things would never be the same between us. Besides, I grew up on the streets." Knives appeared in Milo's hands and then vanished again. "I can take care of myself."

"You're just going to sneak in behind us if I order you to stay here, aren't you?

"Of course. If it makes you feel any better, I would feel guilty over ignoring a direct order."

"Really?"

"No."

"That's what I thought. Okay, you can come, but stay close to me."

Milo smirked, "Oh boy, I get to guard the royal body!"

A genuine smile spread across my face. I turned and climbed down into King Rat's tunnels. The first thing I heard was the unmistakable sound of weapons echoing through the tunnels!

# Chapter 45

*David*

I took a position at the door into the tunnels down which we heard running feet. We had two minutes, give or take, before the tunnel before us filled with tunnel rats.

"Keep an eye on the hole, Martin. I don't think anyone will try to climb up the cage bars like I did, but you never know. Even a one-handed man can guard that spot."

Martin joined me at the door. "Stand aside, Wonder Boy. I've got first dibs on door duty."

"Don't be ridiculous, Martin! You've lost a lot of blood *and* only have one good hand. By what tortured logic are you the right man to defend the door?"

Martin's lips twitched up in a tight smile. "By the logic of expendability. You, David, have too much to lose to even be considered for this job."

I waved the comment off. "I risk my life. You risk your life. The difference is both of my hands are intact and all of my blood is in my veins."

"You also have a beautiful wife who loves you. After everything you've each been through—and, yes, I realize I'm responsible for some of those things—I think the two of you deserve a long and wonderful life together. Besides, you've got the royal succession to think about, lad. I have no doubt you find that an onerous duty, but I'm equally confident you and Callan spend most nights wrestling with this task. Nothing less than the future of the realm depends on you, my boy!"

"Is there anyone in the kingdom who isn't discussing my private life with Callan?"

"It's distinctly possible, David. I feel sure there is a convent or monastery somewhere in Mordan where they restrict themselves to more heavenly matters. Everyone else in the kingdom is speculating whether your first child will be a beautiful little princess or a brave little prince." Martin grinned at me. "I'm hoping for one of each."

I decided it was past time to change the subject. "Okay, I have something to live for. Everyone does—even you!"

"Me? I'm just a former raider whose passing would hardly be noticed. Besides, you've done a lot of Boosting today. Can't have you risking Boost burnout, can we? Safety first, youngster!"

"Would you deprive my unborn children of the chance to meet their Uncle Martin?"

Martin raised a questioning eyebrow. "Uncle?"

"An honorary title, but one bestowed with sincerity."

"Uncle, huh? You make a compelling argument, young man. All right, what's your plan?"

"Thus far, surprise has worked wonders against these tunnel rats. Are you up for a bit more of that, old man?"

"I do believe I could manage that. What do you have in mind?"

"Since you insist on joining the fight, why wait for them to come to us? Let's take the fight to them. If we hit them hard and fast, we might be able to break through their lines and escape into the tunnels."

"It beats hanging around in doorways. Lead on, David!"

We charged down the tunnel toward the approaching guards!

# Chapter 46

*David*

Ahead of us, the tunnel curved curved gently to the right. Echoes made it impossible to gauge how close our enemy was to us using sound, alone. Then I realized flickering light from their torches reflected off the outside wall of the bend in the tunnel. King Rat's men were almost upon us. Dropping our torch, I motioned Martin against the inside wall. Martin ground the torch out under his heel.

In a stage whisper, Martin said, "When the fight is joined, remember to yell 'For Callan and country!'"

There must have been just enough reflected light for him to see my raised eyebrow. "I thought you were raised on adventure vids, David. Don't you know that alliterative declarations of love and loyalty increase fighting prowess?"

I couldn't help but laugh. Through his own pain and exhaustion, Martin still worked to put me at ease. Then, two dozen or more of King Rat's men rounded the bend, charging headlong toward us. As planned, they had no idea we were there until Martin and I stepped into the small pool of torchlight.

I grinned and cried, "For Callan and country!"

Beside me, Martin yelled, "For Martin and Mordan!"

So much for my hopes of learning the name of some hitherto unknown lady love.

*Boost!*

The tunnel rats at the front saw us first. Expressions of alarm crossed their faces and they tried to stop their charge. The dozens behind them didn't see us and shoved the leaders toward us. One impaled himself on Martin's blade. Martin rammed the blade home and it went straight through the leader and into the chest of the man pushing him from behind. The two men shrieked in agony and terror. Finally aware something was amiss at the front, the men behind ground to a halt.

I spun past the two shrieking men and decapitated the third man. His head ricocheted off the wall and into the packed men behind. Cries of horror and disgust rose from them and several back-pedaled from the bouncing head. I grabbed the shirt of the headless man and, using the body as a shield and a psychological weapon, pressed it into the men before me. Hot blood spurted in their faces and they recoiled.

A quick slash to a sword arm and a sword clattered to the floor. A thrust to the leg and a man collapsed against his fellows, unable to stand. Then Martin was back at my side and our blades flashed too fast for King Rat's men to parry.

Our attack was too fast, too unexpected, and we pressed our advantage. The front rank wavered, putting up token resistance. The men at the back, only able to hear the cries from the front, edged away. We had them on the ropes, ready to flee before our onslaught!

Then a man in the middle, close enough to see us but too far away to fight us, regained his senses.

"There's only two of them and one is already wounded. Press forward and grind them under our feet!"

Fear deepened on the faces of the men crossing swords with us, but the rest of their number took the instructions to heart. The mass of tunnel rats advanced. They even adopted one of my tactics, holding the bodies of their slain fellows as shields against our attacks.

Slowly, the inexorable tide of tunnel rats pushed Martin and me back. Martin stumbled from exhaustion and we lost several more steps as I steadied him. Neither of us could hold out much longer.

I blinked back tears of rage and frustration and cried out, "I'm sorry, Callan. I did my best."

# Chapter 47

*Callan*

Despite their squat bodies, trogs can move fast when they want to. The Great One led the way down the tunnels at a run and I was hard pressed to keep up. He'd stop every now and then, listening and sniffing the air, giving me a chance to catch my breath. I don't know if he really could smell anything or if he was just trying to make us think he could, but I appreciated the brief stops. The problem was we didn't seem to be getting any closer to the fighting.

Sound echoed strangely in the tunnels, especially indistinct sounds such as clashing steel. If only someone would yell or call out, the sound might echo differently and help guide us to the fighting.

*"For Callan and country!"*

It was David's voice! He was alive!

*"For Martin and Mordan!"*

Martin was alive, too!

The echoes still made things difficult, but the sound seemed most clear from a tunnel to our right.

"Great One—this way!"

The Great One shouldered his way back to us, sniffed once, then ran up the tunnel. Milo and I stood aside as the rest of the trogs charged off in his wake.

"Callan?"

"Yes, Milo?"

"May I please have permission to laugh at David and Martin for those battle cries?"

"Assuming we all survive the next few minutes, you most definitely have permission. But only if I get to listen in when you make fun of them," I replied. "Do you want to bet on who came up with the idea of the battle cries?"

"Only if I can bet on Martin."

"We can't both bet on Martin, so I guess we won't bet." Then, I fell in behind the last of the trogs and saved my breath for running.

The sounds of battle were growing louder. We were heading in the right direction!

*"There's only two of them and one is already wounded. Press forward and grind them under our feet!"*

Their situation sounded dire. God help me, I couldn't come this close only to lose David in the end!

"Hurry, Great One!"

The Great One nodded and picked up the pace. It felt as if we charged on forever. I suspect it was mere seconds, but they seemed hours long to me. Then I heard a cry which froze my blood.

*"I'm sorry, Callan. I did my best."*

"David Rice, don't you dare die on me!" I yelled as loudly as I could.

A startled reply echoed down the tunnel. "Callan?"

"Damned right it's me, David! And I brought help."

The Great One rounded a bend in the tunnel and gave a ferocious cry of triumph. His trogs joined in as they raised their spears and charged into battle!

*"Trogs!"*

Even over the trog war cry, the terror in that cry was palpable. Screams sounded as the trogs pushed forward, Milo and me right on their heels.

"Tunnel rats, fight on and you will die. Surrender and your life will be spared. You have my word." David's voice rose above the din, calm and commanding.

Another scream sounded.

A sword clattered to the tunnel floor. "I surrender!"

Another sword dropped. "Me, too"

Sword after sword fell, each followed by a cry of surrender. I had feared the trogs would keep killing, but the Great One kept them in check. Within seconds, the fight was over.

And then David pushed through the crowd of trogs and tunnel rats. He swept me into his arms and his lips met mine. I was whole again!

# Chapter 48

*Callan*

David held me tightly, the feel of him and the scent of him overwhelming my senses. Then I realized part of that scent had the sharp, metallic tang of blood. I had been so overjoyed to see David, I hadn't noticed the blood splattering his clothes.

"Darling, how much of this blood is yours?" I asked.

"None of it," he said. "Or not much of it, anyway. I got a few scratches, nothing more."

"Yes, your Wonder Boy is hale and hearty and disgustingly unharmed," drawled Martin from behind David. "That's more than some of us can say. I'd wring my hands in distress, but it would hurt too much and my hand would probably start bleeding again."

I looked around my husband and gasped at the sight of Martin's mangled hand. "Oh my God, Martin! What happened?"

"I discovered that tammars are extremely quick, Your Highness. They also have big, sharp claws."

"We've got to take Martin to Tristan! The *Pauline* is not far from here and Tristan has a surgery setup to handle our wounded warriors." I glanced at the trogs, seeing nothing more than minor cuts and scrapes. "And it looks like Martin is the only one in need of a surgeon."

I took David's hand and started back down the tunnel. David did not come along with me.

"You and Milo take Martin back to the airship and let Tristan get started," David said. "The trogs and I have to finish business down here."

"What do you mean by that?" I asked. "I just got you back, David."

"Callan, David has sworn to kill King Rat," Martin said. "He's got some wild idea about freeing the city-states of the vile little rat boy's influence. You know, typical heroic and noble stuff about making the world a better place blah blah blah. What I find irksome is the lad thinks I'll let him take all the credit simply because a tammar scratched my hand."

"The right word is 'mauled,' Martin," David said.

"You say mauled, I say scratched. Whatever. I entered these tunnels to find you and take you back home," Martin said. "I am not leaving until you leave."

David massaged his forehead. "Why are you being so stubborn, Martin?"

"There's this princess, beautiful but possessed of a fiery temper who–"

"Don't you dare finish that sentence, Martin Bane!" My smile and tone belied my words.

"You're all mad," David sighed. "Fine, Martin, come with me. But Callan, you and Milo–"

"Don't *you* dare finish that sentence, David Rice!" I did not smile and my tone brooked no argument. "If you have got to kill this King Rat, then let's get it over with. The sooner the man is dead, the sooner we can go home!"

David met my gaze for a few seconds then smiled. "As you wish, Your Highness. I'm too tired to argue, anyway."

Milo grinned and gave me a thumb's up. The Great One chuffed, a sound I'd come to recognize as trog laughter.

"Lady Death worthy mate for Hand of Death."

David looked at me. "Lady Death? Hand of Death?"

I patted David's arm. "I'll tell you after we're safely onboard the *Pauline*."

David had the trogs gather the swords dropped by King Rat's men and then ordered those men to lie face down on the floor. He left half a dozen trogs guarding the prisoners and, with a wave of his arm, led us back down the tunnel to find King Rat.

# Chapter 49

*David*

I'd only been in these tunnels for a few days, but I'd obviously missed out on a lot up in the real world. From the way Milo snickered at the Great One's words of approval for Callan, quite a tale awaited me.

The map of the tunnels my implant had constructed didn't stretch into the area where we were. With a little guesswork on my part, I found my way into familiar territory in short order. Now certain of my course, I led the way toward the entrance to the tammar pit. King Rat had been there mere moments ago, so it was the best place to start. If he had wandered off, I felt certain I could find someone who would know where to find him. I was further certain that someone could be convinced to share the king's location with me.

Martin tried to hide it, but he was on the ragged edge of exhaustion. He'd lost a lot of blood and the fight we had just finished had worn him down even further. With every step he took, Martin's breath hissed quietly through clenched teeth. If I was the wounded one, my implant would have flooded my system with analgesics. But the pain killers weren't like adrenaline, which our bodies made and our implants stored. Martin had been on Aashla for fifteen years without access to implant resupply. By now, I doubted he had any analgesics remaining. I had to get Martin back to Tristan for proper medical care as soon as possible.

We swung into the tunnel leading up to the doors to the tammar pit. Two men stood guard. At sight of me, they raised their swords.

One shouted, "Rice is—"

Then the trogs padded into the tunnel behind me. The guards' eyes went wide and the talkative one screamed, "Trogs!"

The two guards bolted down a side tunnel. With the guards out of the way, I prepared to make one heck of an entrance.

"Great One, have two of your warriors slam those doors open as I approach."

The big trog spoke and two of his warriors slipped past me to the doors.

"Callan, please walk at my left side. Oh, and do that regal princess thing you do so well." Callan came to my side, her court posture and countenance settling over her like a favorite gown. I linked arms with her and wished I could match my wife's composure.

I looked over my shoulder. "Milo, please give Martin a steadying hand. It just wouldn't do for him to collapse and spoil our grand entrance!"

With everything in place and everyone ready, we resumed walking. At my signal, the two trogs threw open the doors. They banged against the walls so hard one door cracked. The sound reverberated around the tammar pit. Silence fell and all eyes turned our way. The crossbowmen, my main worry, lounged near the door, their weapons propped against bench seats or lying on the floor.

"King Rat, you have threatened my country, imprisoned my friends, and kept me from my wife. I am tired of your dark, dank tunnels. I am tired of the scum you call subjects. I am tired of *you*."

I pointed my sword at King Rat, who stood rooted in place just outside the tammar cage. "Your kingdom is at an end and your power broken. Life as you have known it is over. Face me. Man to man. Blade to blade. Face me and die like a man!"

# Chapter 50

*David*

The echoes of my challenge faded and still none of the tunnel rats moved or spoke. Then one of the crossbowmen shook himself free of his surprise. With an inarticulate cry of rage, he grabbed his crossbow and tugged on the cocking lever.

The Great One roared and charged past me. He rammed his spear straight through the man and out his back. He lifted his spear over his head, the dying man still impaled upon it, and roared again. With a heave, he flung the body at the feet of the other crossbowmen. He waved the crimson-coated spear before the eyes of the remaining crossbowmen, daring them to attack.

Eyes wide, the men stopped reaching for their weapons. One after another, they raised their hands and backed away from their crossbows.

"What are you doing, you cowards? He's just one trog! He can't kill all of you before some of you shoot him!" King Rat waved his sword toward us. "Attack them! Defend your king!"

The crossbowmen obviously decided they were out of the fight and they showed no interest in getting back into it. They ignored the order and kept backing away. But half a dozen of the king's guards drew swords and charged up the stairs toward the Great One. With a blood-curdling yell, the Great One and his warriors leapt down the stairs to meet them.

The trogs outnumbered the guards three to one and didn't hesitate to take advantage of their superior numbers. The charging trogs encircled the overzealous guards. Lowering their spears, the circle of trogs closed in. Far too late to save themselves, the men came to their senses. Pleas and screams fell on deaf ears. On a command from the Great One, the trogs thrust their spears into the men packed before them. Again and again, the spears thrust until the men within the circle no longer cried or moved.

At my side, Callan paled but watched with resolution.

Seeing me eying her with concern, she said, "These men watched and cheered the slaughter in the tammar pit months ago. They watched and cheered as bound and helpless people were ripped to pieces by the tammar. At the very least, these men held weapons and had the choice to fight or surrender. That is far more than they granted the tammar's victims."

Callan was right. Perhaps this wasn't exactly her culture, but it was her planet. She knew its ways far better than I, who had been here but half a year. I kept my expression impassive and spoke only after the trogs stepped back from the bloody corpses.

"Does anyone else wish to die to defend a king who cowers from combat and watches the slaughter from a safe distance?" I waved my hand toward the trogs. "You all know the trogs' reputation. If you'd rather not face them across the tip of a spear, throw down your weapons *now*. Any who surrender will be spared. Any who still hold weapons ten seconds from now will die."

All around the tammar pit, weapons clattered to the floor.

"Smart move, rats," Martin called. "Now clear the pit floor. I really need a drink right now, but I can't go get one until my friend David kills your king in a fair fight."

# Chapter 51

*Callan*

Tunnel rats backed away from King Rat while Martin's orders still echoed around the tammar pit. The king of the rats spun left and right, looking for support from someone. He called something, anger in his voice.

I turned to Martin. "Do you feel up to translating for me? I don't speak this language and would like to know what's going on."

"I would be honored, Your Highness."

With Martin speaking softly in my ear, I turned back to watch my husband and King Rat.

"Come back here and defend your king. We have a thousand rats in these tunnels. We can destroy them, but only if you defend *me*!"

Walking down the stairs to the pit floor, David shook his head. "You're wasting your breath, Vraal. No one in this room will waste their life defending a dead man."

"You will use my proper title and show proper respect when speaking to me, boy!"

A laugh devoid of all humor escaped David's lips. "You truly are delusional, rat man. I show you more respect than you deserve simply by *speaking* to you. As for proper titles, I can think of many appropriate ones. I will not, however, use such language before my royal wife or my young friend, Milo."

King Rat's eyes blazed with fury and more than a little madness. "I could have killed you the moment you were dragged before me, you know. But I did not. You now owe me the same consideration, Rice."

"Apparently you *are* delusional." David spread his arms and spun in a circle. "You kept me alive for this. I bet you can see the spectacle in your mind. The seats packed with tunnel rats. Four hungry tammars circling the edge of the cage. The warmup victims littering the cage floor, nothing more than mangled corpses. Finally, I am

HENRY VOGEL

dragged into the pit and thrust into the cage. A fitting end to the man who ruined your last great spectacle."

David stopped his slow spin and glared at King Rat.

"*That* is why you kept me alive. *That* is why I'm down here in the first place. You want revenge? Come and take it! You want spectacle? Congratulations, you get to be part of it!"

Regardless of how this duel ended, King Rat's rule was finished. David had shown the man had grown too weak to keep his throne. With my years in court, I could read the tunnel rats as if they wore signs proclaiming their feelings. Did David realize that?

"He's already lost everything, David," I called in Mordanian. "Don't expect rational behavior from him."

Giving me a tired smile and a nod, David turned toward King Rat and, with a flourish, drew his sword. The rest of us spread out around the wall of the pit, ringing the two combatants. The Great One spread his warriors around the circle, insuring none of the tunnel rats interfered in the coming duel.

"Let's get this over with, rat boy" David said, stalking to the center of the circle.

King Rat roared his fear and frustration and anger. Sword held high, he charged at David!

In the blink of an eye, David changed. Quick and graceful to begin with, he grew more graceful, and so much quicker my eye barely saw his sword. He straightened, his weariness washed away before my eyes. As I have done so many times since I first learned the possible dangers of Boost, I fervently prayed this Boost would not kill him.

David blocked King Rat's attack with contemptuous ease. He stepped aside, allowing the man to charge past him, and kicked King Rat in the backside as he ran past. The king stumbled to a halt, his eyes blazing at the insult.

King Rat bent from the waist, clutching at his heart. As soon as David took a single step in the king's direction, the rat spun around, his sword swinging in a wide arc. David simply ducked under the swing. Then, with the flick of a wrist, he slashed open King Rat's sword arm. King Rat's sword dropped to the floor and he clutched his wounded arm. David swung the pommel of his sword across the

236

king's jaw. King Rat collapsed in a heap, cringing and mewling at David's feet.

David shook his head in disgust. "I came down here to kill you so you'd never threaten me or mine again. But now I see you for what you truly are. And what you are is a man so pathetic I won't sully this fine blade with your foul blood. Crawl back to your tunnel rats, Vraal. They can dispose of you."

Weariness settled on him again as David dropped Boost. He turned his back on King Rat and walked toward me. Behind him, King Rat rose to his feet, a dagger raised to plunge into David's unprotected back!

# Chapter 52

*David*

I walked away from the craven rat king, longing to do nothing but wrap Callan in my arms and hold her until this whole affair faded from my mind. Smiling, I reached for Callan. An answering smile spread across her lips and the fear in her eyes faded. Then the fear rushed back into her eyes. She pointed over my shoulder.

*"David!"*

Pushed to the limit by running battles, narrow escapes, and on-again, off-again Boosting, my body was slow to react. Sluggishly, I spun to face whatever threat Callan saw. Martin, standing at Callan's side and suffering from blood loss and exhaustion, was too far away and even slower than I was.

I saw the glint of polished steel.

I saw the white of King Rat's bared teeth.

I saw my death reflected in King Rat's eyes.

I saw the Great One and his trogs watching with great interest. As I understood their customs, this fight belonged to me. They would not dishonor me by interfering.

I saw King Rat lunge toward me. The dagger descending too fast for me to react. If I had a spare second more, I could dodge the blade. But it seemed I had used up my allotment of spare seconds.

In a blur, something small moved between my attacker and me. King Rat screamed as a knife appeared and pierced his wrist. His hand spasmed and the dagger meant for my heart fell to the floor. Shock flooded King Rat's face. He stumbled away, hands clutching at a second knife protruding just below his rib cage. King Rat opened his mouth and blood flowed from it. He coughed once, spraying blood over the small figure between us.

"Leave my family alone!" Milo snarled, the sweet kid I knew so well replaced by the kid forced to fight for survival on the streets of Faroon.

King Rat's eyes rolled up into his head and he fell backward. The body convulsed once and lay still.

Milo spun to face me, concern written on his face. "Are you okay, David? Did I get him before he stabbed you?"

Callan swept past me and pulled Milo into a tight embrace. "Yes, you got him in time. The dagger never touched David. And I can never thank you enough, Milo!"

Then I reached out and joined the embrace.

"So, family, huh?" I asked.

"Um, it just came out wrong. I meant to say friends." Milo didn't meet my eyes.

Callan snorted. "You most certainly did *not* mean to say friends! And, as far as I'm concerned, you *are* family, Milo!"

Milo looked up, tears glistening in his eyes. "Do you really mean that?"

"Of course, we really mean it," I said. "Now, what do you say we get out of these tunnels. I'm ready to see the sky again!"

# Chapter 53

*David*

I turned to the tunnel rats gathered around us. "King Rat is dead. There is nothing left for you down here. It's time to get out of the tunnels and give up this stupid excuse for a life."

Despite everything which had happened in the last few minutes, one of the tunnel rats still managed to dredge up some attitude. "And what if we don't want to leave? What if I want to be the new King Rat?"

"You see those blue guys over there?" I waved my arm toward the band of trogs. "If I hear anyone stayed in these tunnels—much less crowned himself the new king—I will personally lead a few hundred of them into these tunnels. If I have to do that, the only things we'll leave behind are the corpses of every tunnel rat we find."

The man opened his mouth again, but I kept speaking. "And don't think you can hide in the tunnels. I've got a better map of this place than any of you have. No one will escape my wrath."

The Great One spoke to his men, I assume translating my words for them. The trogs all chuffed. They leveled their spears at the man who had spoken and jabbed once. Though well out of range, the man jumped back and the trogs chuffed some more.

"Do you have any other stupid questions?" I asked.

The belligerent one shook his head, eyes wide.

"Then get out of my sight. Spread the word and clear the tunnels."

The tunnel rats backed from the room. Most ran the moment they cleared the door.

"Good threat. Much fun." The Great One jabbed the air with his spear. "Say before, say again. You make good trog."

"Thank you, I guess." I wrapped Martin's good arm over my shoulders, lending him my strength and support. "Come on, let's get out of here."

Ten minutes later, we climbed out of the tunnels. It took some work to get one-handed Martin up the ladder, but we made it without hurting him too badly.

I squinted into the gray light of predawn, thrilled to see the sky again. "Callan tells me you know the way to go, Milo. Please lead on."

Short minutes later, we climbed the stairs to the roof where the *Pauline*—and medical care for Martin—waited for us. Milo reached the rooftop and came to a stop.

"David," he said, "I don't think we're out of this yet."

"Then move so I can come up there and see what you see," I said.

Milo stepped aside, allowing Callan and me to reach the roof. The *Pauline* waited right where Callan said it would be. But ours wasn't the only airship in the area. Fifty feet beyond the roof's edge floated two Beloren warships. Both ships had all their weapons trained on us!

# Chapter 54

*Callan*

David and I stared at the Beloren airships for a moment before he spoke. "I must admit this is an unexpected development."

"I had hoped this wouldn't happen, darling, but I knew it was possible."

"My dear, this is why smart women are so wonderful. As you knew it was possible, please tell me that you made plans for this?"

"Of course I did."

A voice rang out from one of the airships. "I speak Mordanian, so don't think you can just stand there and scheme in your own language!"

I motioned for the trogs to stay on the stairs, out of sight from the Beloren airships, then led David to the edge of the roof.

"Who's in charge here?" I called to the airships.

The man who had spoken earlier said, "I am in charge. Now who are you?"

"David, you're so good at this. Would you mind terribly doing the honors?" I asked.

"Are you kidding? I love this bit." Raising his voice, David called, "You are addressing Her Royal Highness, Princess Callan, Heir to the throne of Mordan. I am her husband, Prince Consort David Rice."

"Ah yes, I've heard of you, Rice," the man replied. "You're the troublemaker."

David drew breath to retort, but I touched his arm. "You don't get to have all the fun, darling. It's my turn."

Drawing forth my royal voice, I said, "If, by troublemaker, you mean the only person within your little city-state who is man enough to fight the tunnel rats in their own territory, then you have the right of it!"

Muttering and spluttering protests rose from both airships. It appeared more than a few of the crew understood Mordanian.

Their captain bristled and called, "I could take you and your friends prisoner right now, little princess!"

"You certainly could try," I shot back. Looking over my shoulder, I called, "Great One, please bring your warriors onto the roof."

Silence fell when the trogs came to stand behind us.

"As you can see, we number rather more than four."

The captain swept his arm in an arc encompassing both airships. "And I *still* outnumber you five or six to one, little princess!"

"Ah, I see you have failed to fully grasp just what these trogs standing before you represent. Indeed, your real problem stems from the trogs standing *behind* you." It was my turn to sweep my arm in a broad arc, one encompassing the southern and western edges of the city. "I suggest you have one of your men turn his spyglass that direction. Look out beyond those fallen walls, the ones you haven't gotten around to rebuilding since my previous visit to your ever-so-welcoming little city."

"Lieutenant?" asked the captain.

The man next to the captain brought the spyglass to his eye and gasped.

"She's not bluffing, sir." The man lowered the spyglass. "The desert is teeming with trogs, sir. There must be hundreds of them."

"Just over a thousand, actually. I don't have the exact number, but just imagine what that many trogs would do to your city-state, *little* captain."

"What do you want, Your Highness?"

"We want to leave, nothing more."

"And what of the trogs surrounding my city?"

"They will leave when we leave. Or they will come in and fetch us if we don't leave by full sunrise. I think that's in about fifteen minutes. Will you require more time than that to come to a decision?"

"No, Your Highness, I will not. You and your companions are free to leave."

I waved the trogs toward the *Pauline.* "Great One, we're leaving, now."

I turned back to the captain. "I suggest you point those weapons in another direction. You wouldn't want your men doing something stupid as we fly away."

Apparently, the captain agreed with me. He was busy issuing orders as David and I boarded the *Pauline*. Tristan, aided by Milo, guided Martin below to the surgery.

Standing in the bow of the little ship and watching the sun rise, I wrapped my arms around David and drew him into a kiss.

"Let's go home, darling.

**ABOUT THE AUTHOR**

**Henry Vogel** had the usual range of menial jobs in his youth before ending up in software QA. Between the menial jobs and the IT jobs, Henry achieved some small fame as a comic book writer and co-creator of the small press titles *Southern Knights* and *X-Thieves*. For the past ten years, Henry has performed all around North Carolina as a professional storyteller. His love of planetary romances can be traced to Mrs. Lashley, a high school math teacher who loaned him her copy of *A Princess of Mars*, fostering a love of the genre which has never died.

Henry currently lives in Raleigh, NC, with his wife, son, two cats, and a host of imaginary friends all clamoring to tell him of their adventures.

\* 9 7 8 1 9 3 8 8 3 4 4 4 8 \*